Mariano Azuela, the first of the "novelists of the Revolution," was born in Lagos de Moreno, Jalisco, Mexico, in 1873. He studied medicine in Guadalajara and returned to Lagos in 1909, where he began the practice of his profession. He began his writing career early; in 1896 he published *Impressions of a Student* in a weekly of Mexico City. This was followed by numerous sketches and short stories, and in 1911 by his first novel, *Andres Perez, maderista*.

Like most of the young Liberals, he supported Francisco I. Madero's uprising, which overthrew the dictatorship of Porfirio Díaz, and in 1911 was made Director of Education of the State of Jalisco. After Madero's assassination, he joined the army of Pancho Villa as doctor, and his knowledge of the Revolution was acquired at firsthand. When the counterrevolutionary forces of Victoriano Huerta were temporarily triumphant, he emigrated to El Paso, Texas, where in 1915 he wrote *The Underdogs* (Los de abajo), which did not receive general recognition until 1924, when it was hailed as *the* novel of the Revolution.

But Azuela was fundamentally a moralist, and his disappointment with the Revolution soon began to manifest itself. He had fought for a better Mexico; but he saw that while the Revolution had corrected certain injustices, it had given rise to others equally deplorable. When he saw the self-servers and the unprincipled turning his hopes for the redemption of the underprivileged of his country into a ladder to serve their own ends, his disillusionment was deep and often bitter. His later novels are marred at times by a savage sarcasm.

During his later years, and until his death in 1952, he lived in Mexico City writing and practicing his profession among the poor.

MARIANO AZUELA

the Underdogs

A Novel of the Mexican Revolution

Translated by E. Munguía, Jr.
Illustrated by J. C. Orozco

With a Foreword by Harriet de Onís

A SIGNET CLASSIC

SIGNET CLASSIC
Published by the Penguin Group
Penguin Books USA Inc., 375 Hudson Street,
New York, New York 10014, U.S.A.
Penguin Books Ltd, 27 Wrights Lane,
London W8 5TZ, England
Penguin Books Australia Ltd, Ringwood,
Victoria, Australia
Penguin Books Canada Ltd, 10 Alcorn Avenue,
Toronto, Ontario, Canada M4V 3B2
Penguin Books (N.Z.) Ltd, 182–190 Wairau Road,
Auckland 10, New Zealand

Penguin Books Ltd, Registered Offices:
Harmondsworth, Middlesex, England

Published by Signet Classic, an imprint of Dutton Signet,
a division of Penguin Books USA Inc.

Original Title: LOS DE ABAJO

First Printing, January, 1963
22 21 20 19 18 17 16 15

Cover painting, "Agrarian Leader Zapata," by Diego Rivera. Courtesy Collection, The Museum of Modern Art, New York. Abby Aldrich Rockefeller Fund.

 REGISTERED TRADEMARK—MARCA REGISTRADA

Printed in the United States of America

FOREWORD

Mexico may be said to have come into being under the sign of revolt. Hernán Cortés and his three hundred companions, for all their bravery and daring, would not have been able to carry out the conquest of the empire of Montezuma, which added to the realm of Charles V greater territories than he had inherited from his Spanish and Hapsburg forebears, without the help of the thousands of Indians of other tribes eager to throw off the yoke of Aztec domination. Cortés himself was a rebel who had embarked on his venture in defiance of the orders of his superior, Governor Velázquez of Cuba. Indeed, his conquest and his life might have been quickly snuffed out, as happened with another rebel, Núñez de Balboa, discoverer of the Pacific, he of the "peak in Darien," if the bulk of the army sent out against Cortés by Velázquez had not preferred to join him rather than fight him.

Mexico's independence pursued a course of its own, apart and separate from the rest of Spanish America. The severing of its links with Spain was followed by years of strife and adversity, among which was the loss of a large part of its territory—Texas, New Mexico, Arizona, California—to the United States, a series of civil wars, and the French invasion which for a brief period turned Mexico into a monarchy with Archduke Maximilian on the throne. It was the Indian Benito Juárez, world famous in his day, who by his dogged, invincible determination assembled almost single-handed the necessary forces to overthrow the emperor, execute him, and by his famous Reform Laws establish liberalism and democracy in Mexico. Unfortunately, his term of office as president was cut short by his death, and an army coup brought to power Porfirio Díaz, who ruled the country as a more or less benevolent dictator for over thirty years. During this period Mexico enjoyed peace, prosperity, and progress, but the benefits therefrom were for a small minority. The poor, the peons on the great haciendas, whose enslavement the Spanish crown had forbidden but who lived in a state of serfdom, the hewers of wood and the drawers of water, were the forgotten people.

It was against this dictatorship that Francisco I. Madero and other liberals and intellectuals led the Revolution of 1910. Among the many revolutions Mexico underwent, this is known as *the* Revolution. It began when the rest of the world was at peace; it ended and consolidated its triumphs while other revolutions, in effect or in the making, were changing the face of history. Not even those who set it in motion and carried it out understood it fully.

When the forces of reaction had been defeated, the struggle began between conflicting ideologies, between the ambitions of the various revolutionary leaders. It cost most of them their lives—Madero, Carranza, Obregón, Zapata, Pancho Villa. The entire country, all social classes, participated in it willy-nilly. The intellectuals who did not flee the country were, almost without exception, on the side of the popular leaders, Zapata or Pancho Villa, with the result that they discovered Mexico.

The colonial epoch of Mexico had been one of great splendor. The Aztec capital, Tenochtitlán, amazed the conquerors by its magnificence and beauty, and on its site Mexico City arose. The churches, palaces, highways the Spaniards built were among the finest of America. Literature flourished; at least two writers of the period stand in the front ranks of Spanish literature: the dramatist Juan Ruíz de Alarcón, and Sor Juana Inés de la Cruz, the Mexican nun, "the tenth muse," one of the greatest woman writers America has produced.

During the nineteenth century the literature and art of Mexico were, for the most part, refined, sophisticated, very European. But out of the Revolution there came a new art, centering about "the underdogs"—mestizos, Indians—their problems, their aspirations, represented by the painting of artists like Diego Rivera, Orozco, Siqueiros, and the literature of the Revolution and post-Revolution, which produced novelists, essayists, poets, of the caliber of Mariano Azuela, Martín Luis Guzmán, José Vasconcelos, Alfonso Reyes, Ramón López Velarde. And at the same time the mother lode of the folk revealed itself in the songs and ballads in which the people wrote their own history of the Revolution, celebrating its heroes, narrating its triumphs and vicissitudes. When the Revolution was over, Mexico had become fused into a homogeneous whole.

The first of the Mexican writers to grasp and give form to the reality of the Revolution was Mariano Azuela. Like Bernal Díaz, one of Cortés' lieutenants and the author of that extraordinary book *The True History of the Conquest of Mexico*, Azuela, too, could say, "That which I myself have seen and the fighting." Born on January 1, 1873, in Lagos de Moreno, Jalisco, he studied medicine in the capital of the state, Guadalajara. During his vacations, traveling about the countryside, spending long periods on the family ranch, he familiarized himself with the types, customs, landscape of the region. He came to know the people of the highlands and the lowlands, listening to them, talking with them. This was the material on which he drew for his novels.

While still young he began to write. His "Impressions of a Student" appeared in a humorous weekly of Mexico City in 1896, and was followed by numerous sketches and short stories. In 1909 he began the practice of medicine in his hometown. Like most of the young liberals, he opposed Porfirio Díaz's bid for reelection, and the following year, with the triumph of Madero, Azuela became the political leader of Lagos, and was appointed Director of Education of the state of Jalisco. After the overthrow and murder of Madero, he was persecuted by the reactionary forces of Victoriano Huerta, and joined the troops of one of Pancho Villa's chieftains, Julián Medina, as a doctor. In this capacity he participated in the fighting in the center and north of Mexico. After Huerta's triumph he emigrated to El Paso, Texas, and it was there in 1915 that he wrote *The Underdogs*. At the time of its publication it went almost unnoticed. It was not until 1924, as the result of a series of articles on the Mexican novel and the Revolution in *El Universal Ilustrado* of Mexico City, that the work achieved recognition. It was published in installments in that weekly, and this was quickly followed by six editions of the novel in Spanish, and its translation into English, French, German, Japanese, Serbian, Russian, Yiddish, and Italian. The author himself adapted his work for the stage, and a film version of it was also made.

Naturally, in the limited scope of this short novel, Azuela could not give the vast chaotic panorama of the struggle in which Mexico was engulfed for so many years. Nor did he attempt to. As the Spanish proverb says: "As a sample, a button will do." The incidents he describes, the atmosphere he creates, were the pattern which repeated itself throughout the country, like images endlessly reflected in facing mirrors. One need only read Martín Luis Guzmán's *The Eagle and the Serpent,* that enthralling narrative of his own revolutionary experiences, to see that fiction and reality were almost indistinguishable. The protagonists of the Revolution were, with rare exceptions, counterparts of Azuela's hero, poor illiterate peasants, often turned outlaw because of clashes with the authorities or the police, and who, gathering to themselves others of their own kind, threw themselves into the struggle with only a dim perception of the objectives involved. Demetrio Macías is a bewildered actor on a stage so multiform as to make his role almost meaningless. When after two years he returns briefly to his little ranch and his wife asks him: "Why do you keep on fighting, Demetrio?" he answers, tossing a pebble into the depths of a canyon: "Look at that stone, how it keeps on going. . . ."

There was a quality of candor and innocence about the early revolutionary figures. Francisco I. Madero ingenuously believed that a revised constitution with a no-reelection proviso would right the country's ills. Men like Zapata or Pancho Villa, for all their primitiveness and brutality, put their good faith and their lives at the service of the aims proclaimed by the intellectual architects of the Revolution. And the peasants who made up their armies, like Demetrio Macías and his followers, totally ignorant of the French Revolution, were living their Mexican version of "Arise ye

prisoners of starvation" without ever having heard the name
of Karl Marx—their songs were "La Adelita" or "La
Valentina," that light, sinister music to which men have
always marched to their death, as Hemingway puts it.
Theirs was an autochthonous uprising, springing from cen-
turies of servitude, exploitation, humiliation, affording an
opportunity to settle long scores with landowners, masters,
and the forces of authority, which they looked upon as
agents of the ruling class. To the cry of "Let's go with
Pancho Villa" they threw off, temporarily at least, the yoke
of their galling submission, and sated old rancors and re-
pressions in pillaging, drinking, raping, fighting, and dying,
going to their death with only a vague notion of what they
were dying for.

One of the remarkable features of Azuela's novel is that
he should so early have grasped two of the human forces at
work in the Revolution: its blind creators and those to
whom the Revolution would be the ladder by which they
mounted to success as typified by Luis Cervantes, the educated city man, who discerned in the rabble in arms the
wave of the future. ". . . revolutionists or bandits, call them
what you will, were going to depose the government," he
mused. "Tomorrow would therefore belong wholly to them.
A man must consequently be on their side, only on their
side. No," he said to himself almost aloud, "I don't think
I've made a mistake this time."

He then proceeds to elucidate to Demetrio and his companions, who listen in rapt admiration and total bewilderment, the goals of the Revolution: "You are a modest man
without ambitions, you do not wish to realize the exceedingly important role you are destined to play. . . . It is not
true that you took up arms simply because of Señor Mónico.
You are under arms to protest against the evils of all the
caciques who are overrunning the whole nation. . . . We are
the tools Destiny makes use of to reclaim the sacred rights
of the people. . . . What moves us is what men call ideals;
our action is what men call fighting for a principle. . . ."

"Pancracio," Macías called, "pull down two more beers."

"It is curious," writes the gifted young Uruguayan critic
Emir Rodríguez Monegal, "that this writer who was one of

the first to join the revolutionary movement, once it had
triumphed withdrew from it more and more. The truth of
the matter is that the Revolution had been withdrawing from
those who began it. . . . In his early novels, such as *The
Underdogs,* he conveyed all that was noble and spontaneous
in the revolution, but at the same time he pointed out . . .
the medium it provided for the culture of demagoguery.
And as soon as the struggle came to an end and sought to
establish order—even though at the cost of compromises
and injustices—Azuela turned his back upon it and became
the chronicler of its defects. . . . The point is that Azuela
is not a reactionary but a moralist. And for that reason he
refuses to tolerate the imperfections of the world. He does
not tolerate them because he, too, around 1910, believed
that the blood shed on the fields of battle and the elimina-
tion of those who had wielded power from above were the
direct methods of solving all injustices and bringing about
the kingdom of happiness on earth. . . . And what Azuela
saw was that one corruption was being substituted by
another, the violence of the 'top dogs' by that of the 'underdogs.' . . . His novels that followed *The Underdogs* have
become the most outspoken denunciation of the moral
reality which underlies and overlies the great revolutionary
achievements of Mexico."

In spite of the abundance of his subsequent writings,
Azuela's fame rests on *The Underdogs*. It is not only that
in it he gives us his vivid firsthand impressions of the Revolution long before any other writer had employed the theme,
transmitting them with the intensity of the moment in which
he experienced them, but also that he so quickly sensed
the problems inherent in its triumph. The strength of the
work lies in its terseness and rapidity; the characters live
with indomitable vitality, and throughout the book one
feels the pulsating breath of beings who are heroes, or at
any rate can behave heroically, without being aware of it.

"If one were to select a single note characteristic of all
Azuela's work," says González de Mendoza, "it would be
this: he fought generously and gallantly against stupid evil
and injustice. Unfortunately, the struggle between intelligence and stupidity, as between rectitude and iniquity, will
probably last as long as mankind endures upon the earth."

Withdrawn from public affairs, Mariano Azuela spent the rest of his long life writing, bringing out a new book almost yearly—novels, short stories, criticism, essays—and practicing his profession among the poor of a humble quarter of Mexico City. His position as one of Mexico's foremost novelists was firmly established. He died on March 1, 1952, and is buried in the Rotonda de Hombres Ilustres, Mexico's Westminster Abbey.

Harriet de Onís

PART ONE

"How beautiful the revolution! Even in its most barbarous aspect it is beautiful," Solís said with deep feeling.

I

THAT'S no animal, I tell you! Listen to the dog barking! It *must* be a human being."

The woman stared into the darkness of the sierra.

"What if they're soldiers?" said a man, who sat Indian-fashion, eating, a coarse earthenware plate in his right hand, three folded tortillas in the other.

The woman made no answer, all her senses directed outside the hut. The beat of horses' hoofs rang in the quarry nearby. The dog barked again, louder and more angrily.

"Well, Demetrio, I think you had better hide, all the same."

Stolidly, the man finished eating; next he reached for a *cántaro* and gulped down the water in it; then he stood up.

"Your rifle is under the mat," she whispered.

A tallow candle illumined the small room. In one corner stood a plow, a yoke, a goad, and other agricultural implements. Ropes hung from the roof, securing an old adobe mold, used as a bed; on it a child slept, covered with gray rags.

Demetrio buckled his cartridge belt about his waist

14

and picked up his rifle. He was tall and well built, with a sanguine face and beardless chin; he wore shirt and trousers of white cloth, a broad Mexican hat and leather sandals.

With slow, measured step, he left the room, vanishing into the impenetrable darkness of the night.

The dog, excited to the point of madness, had jumped over the corral fence.

Suddenly a shot rang out. The dog moaned, then barked no more. Some men on horseback rode up, shouting and swearing; two of them dismounted, while the other hung back to watch the horses.

"Hey, there, woman: we want food! Give us eggs, milk, beans, anything you've got! We're starving!"

"Curse the sierra! It would take the Devil himself not to lose his way!"

"Guess again, Sergeant! Even the Devil would go astray if he were as drunk as you are."

The first speaker wore chevrons on his arm, the other red stripes on his shoulders.

"Whose place is this, old woman? Or is it an empty house? God's truth, which is it?"

"Of course it's not empty. How about the light and that child there? Look here, confound it, we want to eat, and damn quick too! Are you coming out or are we going to make you?"

"You swine! Both of you! You've gone and killed my dog, that's what you've done! What harm did he ever do you? What did you have against *him?*"

The woman reentered the house, dragging the dog behind her, very white and fat, with lifeless eyes and flabby body.

"Look at those cheeks, Sergeant! Don't get riled, light of my life: I swear I'll turn your home into a dovecot, see?"

"By God!" he said, breaking off into song:

> *"Don't look so haughty, dear,*
> *Banish all fears,*
> *Kiss me and melt to me,*
> *I'll drink up your tears!"*

His alcoholic tenor trailed off into the night.

"Tell me what they call this ranch, woman?" the sergeant asked.

"Limón," the woman replied curtly, carrying wood to the fire and fanning the coals.

"So we're in Limón, eh, the famous Demetrio Macías' country, eh? Do you hear that, Lieutenant? We're in Limón."

"Limón? What the hell do I care? If I'm bound for hell, Sergeant, I might as well go there now. I don't mind, now that I've found as good a remount as this! Look at the cheeks on the darling, look at them! There's a pair of ripe red apples for a fellow to bite into!"

"I'll wager you know Macías the bandit, lady? I was in the pen with him at Escobedo, once."

"Bring me a bottle of tequila, Sergeant: I've decided to spend the night with this charming lady. . . . What's that? The colonel? . . . Why in God's name talk about the colonel now? He can go straight to hell, for all I care. And if he doesn't like it, it's all right with me. Come on, Sergeant, tell the corporal outside to unsaddle the horses and feed them. I'll stay here all night. Here, my girl, you let the sergeant fry the eggs and warm up the tortillas; you come here to me. See this wallet full of nice new bills? They're all for you, darling. Sure, I want you to have them. Figure it out for yourself. I'm drunk, see: I've a bit of a load on and that's why I'm kind of hoarse, you might call it. I left half my gullet down Guadalajara way, and I've been spitting the other half out all the way up here. Oh well, who cares? But I want you to have that money, see, dearie? Hey, Sergeant, where's my bottle? Now, little girl, come here and pour yourself a drink. You won't, eh? Aw, come on! Afraid of your—er—husband . . . or whatever he is, huh? Well, if he's skulking in some hole, you tell him to come out. What the hell do I care? I'm not scared of rats, see!"

Suddenly a white shadow loomed on the threshold.

"Demetrio Macías!" the sergeant cried as he stepped back in terror.

The lieutenant stood up, silent, cold and motionless as a statue.

"Shoot them!" the woman croaked.

"Oh, come, you'll surely spare us! I didn't know you were there. I'll always stand up for a brave man."

Demetrio stood his ground, looking them up and down, an insolent and disdainful smile wrinkling his face.

"Yes, I not only respect brave men, but I like them. I'm proud and happy to call them friends. Here's my hand on it: friend to friend." Then, after a pause: "All right, Demetrio Macías, if you don't want to shake hands, all right! But it's because you don't know me, that's why, just because the first time you saw me I was doing this dog's job. But look here, I ask you, what in God's name can a man do when he's poor and has a wife to support and kids? . . . Right you are, Sergeant, let's go: I've nothing but respect for the home of what I call a brave man, a real, honest, genuine man!"

When they had gone, the woman drew close to Demetrio.

"Holy Virgin, what agony! I suffered as though it was you they'd shot."

"You go to father's house, quick!" Demetrio ordered. She wanted to hold him in her arms; she entreated, she wept. But he pushed away from her gently and, in a sullen voice, said, "I've an idea the whole lot of them are coming."

"Why didn't you kill 'em?"

"Their hour hasn't struck yet."

They went out together; she bore the child in her arms. At the door, they separated, moving off in different directions.

The moon peopled the mountain with vague shadows. As he advanced at every turn of his way Demetrio could see the poignant, sharp silhouette of a woman pushing forward painfully, bearing a child in her arms.

When, after many hours of climbing, he gazed back, huge flames shot up from the depths of the canyon by the river. It was his house, blazing. . . .

II

EVERYTHING was still swathed in shadows as Demetrio Macías began his descent to the bottom of the ravine. Between rocks striped with huge eroded cracks, and a squarely cut wall, with the river flowing below, a narrow ledge along the steep incline served as a mountain trail.

"They'll surely find me now and track us down like dogs," he mused. "It's a good thing they know nothing about the trails and paths up here. . . . But if they got someone from Moyahua to guide them . . ." He left the sinister thought unfinished. "All the men from Limón or Santa Rosa or the other nearby ranches are on our side: they wouldn't try to trail us. That *cacique* who's chased and run me ragged over these hills, is at Mohayua now; he'd give his eyeteeth to see me dangling from a telegraph pole with my tongue hanging out of my mouth, purple and swollen. . . ."

At dawn, he approached the pit of the canyon. Here, he lay on the rocks and fell asleep.

The river crept along, murmuring as the waters rose and fell in small cascades. Birds sang lyrically from their hiding among the *pitaya* trees. The monotonous, eternal drone of insects filled the rocky solitude with mystery.

Demetrio awoke with a start. He waded the river, following its course which ran counter to the canyon; he climbed the crags laboriously as an ant, gripping root and rock with his hands, clutching every stone in the trail with his bare feet.

When he reached the summit, he glanced down to see the sun steeping the valley in a lake of gold. Near the canyon, enormous rocks loomed protrudent, like fantastic Negro skulls. The *pitaya* trees rose tenuous, tall, like the tapering, gnarled fingers of a giant; other trees of all sorts

18

bowed their crests toward the pit of the abyss. Amid
the stark rocks and dry branches, roses bloomed like a
white offering to the sun as smoothly, suavely, it unrav-
eled its golden threads, one by one, from rock to rock.

Demetrio stopped at the summit. Reaching backward,
with his right arm he drew his horn which hung at his
back, held it up to his thick lips, and, swelling his cheeks
out, blew three loud blasts. From across the hill close by,
three sharp whistles answered his signal.

In the distance, from a conical heap of reeds and dry
straws, man after man emerged, one after the other, their
legs and chests naked, lambent and dark as old bronze.
They rushed forward to greet Demetrio, and stopped before him, askance.

"They've burnt my house," he said.

A murmur of oaths, imprecations, and threats rose
among them.

Demetrio let their anger run its course. Then he drew
a bottle from under his shirt and took a deep swig;
then he wiped the neck of the bottle with the back of his
hand and passed it around. It passed from mouth to
mouth; not a drop was left. The men passed their tongues
greedily over their lips to recapture the tang of the liquor.

"Glory be to God and by His Will," said Demetrio,
"tonight or tomorrow at the latest we'll meet the Federals.
What do you say, boys, shall we let them find their way
about these trails?"

The ragged crew jumped to their feet, uttering shrill
cries of joy; then their jubilation turned sinister and they
gave vent to threats, oaths and imprecations.

"Of course, we can't tell how strong they are," said
Demetrio as his glance traveled over their faces in
scrutiny.

"Do you remember Medina? Out there at Hos-
totipaquillo, he only had a half a dozen men with knives
that they sharpened on a grindstone. Well, he held back
the soldiers and the police, didn't he? And he beat them,
too."

"We're every bit as good as Medina's crowd!" said a
tall, broad-shouldered man with a black beard and bushy
eyebrows.

"By God, if I don't own a Mauser and a lot of cartridges, if I can't get a pair of trousers and shoes, then my name's not Anastasio Montáñez! Look here, Quail, you don't believe it, do you? You ask my partner Demetrio if I haven't half a dozen bullets in me already. Christ! Bullets are marbles to me! And I dare you to contradict me!"

"Viva Anastasio Montáñez," shouted Manteca.

"All right, all right!" said Montáñez. "Viva Demetrio Macías, our chief, and long life to God in His heaven and to the Virgin Mary."

"Viva Demetrio Macías," they all shouted.

They gathered dry brush and wood, built a fire and placed chunks of fresh meat upon the burning coals. As the blaze rose, they collected about the fire, sat down Indian-fashion and inhaled the odor of the meat as it twisted on the crackling fire. The rays of the sun, falling about them, cast a golden radiance over the bloody hide of a calf, lying on the ground nearby. The meat dangled from a rope fastened to a *huizache* tree, to dry in the sun and wind.

"Well, men," Demetrio said, "you know we've only twenty rifles, besides my thirty-thirty. If there are just a few of them, we'll shoot until there's not a live man left. If there's a lot of 'em, we can give 'em a good scare, anyhow."

He undid a rag belt about his waist, loosened a knot in it and offered the contents to his companions. Salt. A murmur of approbation rose among them as each took a few grains between the tips of his fingers.

They ate voraciously; then, glutted, lay down on the ground, facing the sky. They sang monotonous, sad songs, uttering a strident shout after each stanza.

III

In the brush and foliage of the sierra, Demetrio Macías and his threescore men slept until the halloo of the horn, blown by Pancracio from the crest of a peak, awakened them.

"Time, boys! Look around and see what's what!" Anastasio Montáñez said, examining his rifle springs. Yet he was previous; an hour or more elapsed with no sound or stir save the song of the locust in the brush or the frog stirring in his mudhole. At last, when the ultimate faint rays of the moon were spent in the rosy dimness of the dawn, the silhouette of a soldier loomed at the end of the trail. As they strained their eyes, they could distinguish others behind him, ten, twenty, a hundred. . . . Then, suddenly, darkness swallowed them up. Only when the sun rose, Demetrio's band realized that the canyon was alive with men, midgets seated on miniature horses.

"Look at 'em, will you?" said Pancracio. "Pretty, ain't they? Come on, boys, let's go and roll marbles with 'em."

Now the moving dwarf figures were lost in the dense chaparral, now they reappeared, stark and black against the ocher. The voices of officers, as they gave orders, and soldiers, marching at ease, were clearly audible.

Demetrio raised his hand; the locks of rifles clicked.

"Fire!" he cried tensely.

Twenty-one men shot as one; twenty-one soldiers fell off their horses. Caught by surprise, the column halted, etched like bas-reliefs in stone against the rocks.

Another volley and a score of soldiers hurtled down from rock to rock.

"Come out, bandits. Come out, you starved dogs!"

"To hell with you, you corn rustlers!"

"Kill the cattle thieves! Kill 'em!"

The soldiers shouted defiance to their enemies; the latter, giving proof of a marksmanship which had already made them famous, were content to keep under cover, quiet, mute.

"Look, Pancracio," said Meco, completely black save for his eyes and teeth. "This is for that man who passes that tree. I'll get the son of a . . ."

"Take that! Right in the head. You saw it, didn't you, mate? Now, this is for the fellow on the roan horse. Down you come, you shave-headed bastard!"

"I'll give that lad on the trail's edge a shower of lead. If you don't hit the river, I'm a liar! Now: look at him!"

"Oh, come on, Anastasio, don't be cruel; lend me your rifle. Come along, one shot, just one!"

Manteca and Quail, unarmed, begged for a gun as a boon, imploring permission to fire at least a shot apiece.

"Come out of your holes if you've got any guts!"

"Show your faces, you lousy cowards!"

From peak to peak, the shouts rang as distinctly as though uttered across a street. Suddenly, Quail stood up, naked, holding his trousers to windward as though he were a bullfighter flaunting a red cape, and the soldiers below the bull. A shower of shots peppered upon Demetrio's men.

"God! That was like a hornet's nest buzzing overhead," said Anastasio Montáñez, lying flat on the ground without daring to wink an eye.

"Here, Quail, you son of a bitch, you stay where I told you," roared Demetrio.

They crawled to take new positions. The soldiers, congratulating themselves on their successes, ceased firing when another volley roused them.

"More coming!" they shouted.

Some, panic-stricken, turned their horses back; others, abandoning their mounts, began to climb up the mountain and seek shelter behind the rocks. The officers had to shoot at them to enforce discipline.

"Down there, down there!" said Demetrio as he leveled his rifle at the translucent thread of the river.

A soldier fell into the water; at each shot, invariably a soldier bit the dust. Only Demetrio was shooting in that direction; for every soldier killed, ten or twenty of them, intact, climbed afresh on the other side.

"Get those coming up from under! *Los de Abajo!* Get the underdogs!" he screamed.

Now his fellows were exchanging rifles, laughing and making wagers on their marksmanship.

"My leather belt if I miss that head there, on the black horse!"

"Lend me your rifle, Meco."

"Twenty Mauser cartridges and a half yard of sausage if you let me spill that lad riding the bay mare. All right! Watch me. . . . There! See him jump! Like a bloody deer."

"Don't run, you half-breeds. Come along with you! Come and meet Father Demetrio!"

Now it was Demetrio's men who screamed insults. Manteca, his smooth face swollen in exertion, yelled his lungs out. Pancracio roared, the veins and muscles in his neck dilated, his murderous eyes narrowed to two evil slits.

Demetrio fired shot after shot, constantly warning his men of impending danger, but they took no heed until they felt the bullets spattering them from one side.

"Goddamn their souls, they've branded me!" Demetrio cried, his teeth flashing.

Then, very swiftly, he slid down a gully and was lost. . . .

IV

TWO men were missing, Serapio the candymaker, and Antonio, who played the cymbals in the Juchipila band.

"Maybe they'll join us further on," said Demetrio.

The return journey proved moody. Anastasio Montáñez alone preserved his equanimity, a kindly expression playing in his sleepy eyes and on his bearded face. Pancracio's harsh, gorillalike profile retained its repulsive immutability.

The soldiers had retreated; Demetrio began the search for the soldiers' horses which had been hidden in the sierra.

Suddenly Quail, who had been walking ahead, shrieked. He had caught sight of his companions swinging from the branches of a mesquite. There could be no doubt of their identity; Serapio and Antonio they certainly were. Anastasio Montáñez prayed brokenly.

"Our Father Who art in heaven, hallowed be Thy name. Thy kingdom come . . ."

"Amen," his men answered in low tones, their heads bowed, their hats upon their breasts. . . .

Then, hurriedly, they took the Juchipila canyon northward, without halting to rest until nightfall.

Quail kept walking close to Anastasio, unable to banish from his mind the two who were hanged, their dislocated limp necks, their dangling legs, their arms pendulous, and their bodies moving slowly in the wind.

On the morrow, Demetrio complained bitterly of his wound; he could no longer ride on horseback. They were forced to carry him the rest of the way on a makeshift stretcher of leaves and branches.

"He's bleeding frightfully," said Anastasio Montáñez, tearing off one of his shirt-sleeves and tying it tightly about Demetrio's thigh, a little above the wound.

"That's good," said Venancio. "It'll keep him from bleeding and stop the pain."

Venancio was a barber. In his native town, he pulled teeth and fulfilled the office of medicine man. He was accorded an unimpeachable authority because he had read *The Wandering Jew* and one or two other books. They called him "Doctor"; and since he was conceited about his knowledge, he employed very few words.

They took turns, carrying the stretcher in relays of four over the bare stony mesa and up the steep passes.

At high noon, when the reflection of the sun on the calcareous soil burned their shoulders and made the landscape dimly waver before their eyes, the monotonous, rhythmical moan of the wounded rose in unison with the ceaseless cry of the locusts. They stopped to rest at every small hut they found hidden between the steep, jagged rocks.

"Thank God, a kind soul and tortillas full of beans and chili are never lacking," Anastasio Montáñez said with a triumphant belch.

The mountaineers would shake calloused hands with the travelers, saying:

"God's blessing on you! He will find a way to help you all, never fear. We're going ourselves, starting tomorrow morning. We're dodging the draft, with those damned Government people who've declared war to the death on us, on all the poor. They come and steal our pigs, our chickens and corn, they burn our homes and carry our women off, and if they ever get hold of us they'll kill us like mad dogs, and we die right there on the spot and that's the end of the story!"

At sunset, amid the flames dyeing the sky with vivid, variegated colors, they descried a group of houses up in the heart of the blue mountains. Demetrio ordered them to carry him there.

These proved to be a few wretched straw huts, dispersed all over the river slopes, between rows of young sprouting corn and beans. They lowered the stretcher and Demetrio, in a weak voice, asked for a glass of water.

Groups of squalid Indians sat in the dark pits of the huts, men with bony chests, disheveled, matted hair, and ruddy cheeks; behind them, eyes shone up from floors of fresh reeds.

A child with a large belly and glossy dark skin came close to the stretcher to inspect the wounded man. An old woman followed, and soon all of them drew about Demetrio in a circle.

A girl sympathizing with him in his plight brought a *jícara* of bluish water. With hands shaking, Demetrio took it up and drank greedily.

"Will you have some more?"

He raised his eyes and glanced at the girl, whose features were common but whose voice had a note of kindness in it. Wiping his sweating brow with the back of his palm and turning on one side, he gasped:

"May God reward you."

Then his whole body shook, making the leaves of the stretcher rustle. Fever possessed him; he fainted.

"It's a damp night and that's terrible for the fever," said Remigia, an old wrinkled barefooted woman, wearing a cloth rag for a blouse.

She invited them to move Demetrio into her hut.

Pancracio, Anastasio Montáñez, and Quail lay down beside the stretcher like faithful dogs, watchful of their master's wishes. The rest scattered about in search of food.

Remigia offered them all she had, chili and tortillas.

"Imagine! I had eggs, chickens, even a goat and her kid, but those damn soldiers wiped me out clean."

Then, making a trumpet of her hands, she drew near Anastasio and murmured in his ear:

"Imagine, they even carried away Señora Nieves' little girl!"

V

Suddenly awakening, Quail opened his eyes and stood up.

"Montáñez, did you hear? A shot, Montáñez! Hey, Montáñez, get up!"

He shook him vigorously until Montáñez ceased snoring and in turn woke up.

"What in the name of . . . Now you're at it again, damn it. I tell you there aren't ghosts any more," Anastasio muttered out of a half-sleep.

"I heard a shot, Montáñez!"

"Go back to sleep, Quail, or I'll bust your nose."

"Hell, Anastasio, I tell you it's no nightmare. I've forgotten those fellows they hung, honest. It's a shot, I tell you. I heard it all right."

"A shot, you say? All right, then, hand me my gun."

Anastasio Montáñez rubbed his eyes, stretched out his arms and legs, and stood up lazily.

They left the hut. The sky was solid with stars; the moon rose like a sharp scythe. The confused rumor of women crying in fright resounded from the various huts; the men who had been sleeping in the open, also woke up and the rattle of arms echoed over the mountain.

"You cursed fool, you've maimed me for life."

A voice rang clearly through the darkness.

"Who goes there?"

The shout echoed from rock to rock, through mound and over hollow, until it spent itself at the far, silent reaches of the night.

"Who goes there?" Anastasio repeated his challenge lounder, pulling back the lock of his Mauser.

"One of Demetrio's men," came the answer.

"It's Pancracio," Quail cried joyfully. Relieved, he rested the butt of his rifle on the ground.

29

Pancracio appeared, holding a young man by the arms; the newcomer was covered with dust from his felt hat to his coarse shoes. A fresh bloodstain lay on his trousers close to the heel.

"Who's this tenderfoot?" Anastasio demanded.

"You know I'm on guard around here. Well, I hears a noise in the brush, see, and I shouts, 'Who goes there?' and then this lad answers, 'Carranza! Carranza!' I don't know anyone by that name, and so I says, 'Carranza, hell!' and I just pumps a bit of lead into his hoof."

Smiling, Pancracio turned his beardless head around as if soliciting applause.

Then the stranger spoke:

"Who's your commander?"

Proudly, Anastasio raised his head, went up to him and looked him in the face. The stranger lowered his tone considerably.

"Well, I'm a revolutionist, too, you know. The Government drafted me and I served as a private, but I managed to desert during the battle the day before yesterday, and I've been walking about in search of you all."

"So he's a Government soldier, eh?" A murmur of incredulity rose from the men, interrupting the stranger.

"So that's what you are, eh? One of those damn half-breeds," said Anastasio Montáñez. "Why the hell didn't you pump your lead in his brain, Pancracio?"

"What's he talking about, anyhow? I can't make head nor tail of it. He says he wants to see Demetrio and that he's got plenty to say to him. But that's all right: we've got plenty of time to do anything we damn well please so long as you're in no hurry, that's all," said Pancracio, loading his gun.

"What kind of beasts are you?" the prisoner cried. He could say no more: Anastasio's fist, crashing down upon his face, sent his head turning on his neck, covered with blood.

"Shoot the half-breed!"

"Hang him!"

"Burn him alive; he's a lousy Federal."

In great excitement, they yelled and shrieked and were about to fire at the prisoner.

"Sssh! Shut up! I think Demetrio's talking now," Anastasio said, striving to quiet them. Indeed, Demetrio, having ascertained the cause of the turmoil, ordered them to bring the prisoner before him.

"It's positively infamous, señor; look," Luis Cervantes said, pointing to the bloodstains on his trousers and to his bleeding face.

"All right, all right. But who in hell are you? That's what I want to know," Demetrio said.

"My name is Luis Cervantes, sir. I'm a medical student and a journalist. I wrote a piece in favor of the revolution, you see; as a result, they persecuted me, caught me, and finally landed me in the barracks."

His ensuing narrative was couched in terms of such detail and expressed in terms so melodramatic that it drew guffaws of mirth from Pancracio and Manteca.

"All I've tried to do is to make myself clear on this point. I want you to be convinced that I am truly one of your coreligionists. . . ."

"What's that? What did you say? Car . . . what?" Demetrio asked, bringing his ear close to Cervantes.

"Coreligionist, sir, that is to say, a person who possesses the same religion, who is inspired by the same ideals, who defends and fights for the same cause you are now fighting for."

Demetrio smiled:

"What *are* we fighting for? That's what I'd like to know."

In his disconcertment, Luis Cervantes could find no reply.

"Look at that mug, look at 'im! Why waste any time, Demetrio? Let's shoot him," Pancracio urged impatiently.

Demetrio laid a hand on his hair which covered his ears, and stretching himself out for a long time, seemed to be lost in thought. Having found no solution, he said:

"Get out, all of you; it's aching again. Anastasio, put out the candle. Lock him up in the corral and let Pancracio and Manteca watch him. Tomorrow, we'll see. . . ."

VI

THROUGH the shadows of the starry night, Luis Cervantes had not yet managed to detect the exact shape of the objects about him. Seeking the most suitable resting-place, he laid his weary bones down on a fresh pile of manure under the blurred mass of a *huizache* tree. He lay down, more exhausted than resigned, and closed his eyes, resolutely determined to sleep until his fierce keepers or the morning sun, burning his ears, awakened him. Something vaguely like warmth at his side, then a tired hoarse breath, made him shudder. He opened his eyes and feeling about him with his hands, he sensed the coarse hairs of a large pig which, resenting the presence of a neighbor, began to grunt.

All Luis' efforts to sleep proved quite useless, not only because the pain of his wound or the bruises on his flesh smarted, but because he suddenly realized the exact nature of his failure.

Yes, failure! For he had never learned to appreciate exactly the difference between fulminating sentences of death upon bandits in the columns of a small country newspaper and actually setting out in search of them, and tracking them to their lairs, gun in hand. During his first day's march as volunteer lieutenant, he had begun to suspect the error of his ways—a brutal sixty miles' journey it was, that left his hips and legs one mass of raw soreness and soldered all his bones together. A week later, after his first skirmish against the rebels, he understood every rule of the game. Luis Cervantes would have taken up a crucifix and solemnly sworn that as soon as the soldiers, gun in hand, stood ready to shoot, some profoundly eloquent voice had spoken behind them, saying, "Run for your lives." It was all crystal clear. Even his noble-spirited horse, accustomed to battle, sought to sweep back on its hind legs and gallop furiously away, to stop only at a safe distance from the sound of firing. The sun was setting, the mountain became peopled with vague and restless shadows, darkness scaled the ramparts of the mountain hastily. What could be more logical then, than to seek refuge behind the rocks and attempt to sleep, granting mind and body a sorely needed rest?

But the soldier's logic is the logic of absurdity. On the morrow, for example, his colonel awakened him rudely out of his sleep, cuffing and belaboring him unmercifully, and, after having bashed in his face, deprived him of his place of vantage. The rest of the officers, moreover, burst into hilarious mirth and holding their sides with laughter begged the colonel to pardon the deserter. The colonel, therefore, instead of sentencing him to be shot, kicked his buttocks roundly for him and assigned him to kitchen police.

This signal insult was destined to bear poisonous fruit. Luis Cervantes determined to play turncoat; indeed, mentally, he had already changed sides. Did not the sufferings of the underdogs, of the disinherited masses, move him to the core? Henceforth he espoused the cause of Demos, of the subjugated, the beaten and baffled, who implore justice, and justice alone. He became intimate with the humblest private. More, even, he shed tears of compassion over a dead mule which fell, load and all, after a terribly long journey.

From then on, Luis Cervantes' prestige with the soldiers increased. Some actually dared to make confessions. One among them, conspicuous for his sobriety and silence, told him: "I'm a carpenter by trade, you know. I had a mother, an old woman nailed to her chair for ten years by rheumatism. In the middle of the night, they pulled me out of my house; three damn policemen; I woke up a soldier twenty-five miles away from my hometown. A month ago our company passed by there again. My mother was already under the sod! . . . So there's nothing left for me in this wide world; no one misses me now, you see. But, by God, I'm damned if I'll use these cartridges they make us carry, against the enemy. If a miracle happens (I pray for it every night,

you know, and I guess our Lady of Guadalupe can do
it all right), then I'll join Villa's men; and I swear by the
holy soul of my old mother, that I'll make every one of
these Government people pay, by God I will."

Another soldier, a bright young fellow, but a charlatan
at heart, who drank habitually and smoked the narcotic
marihuana weed, eyeing him with vague, glassy stare,
whispered in his ear, "You know, partner . . . the men
on the other side . . . you know, the other side . . . you
understand . . . they ride the best horses up north there,
and all over, see? And they harness their mounts with
pure hammered silver. But us? Oh hell, we've got to ride
plugs, that's all, and not one of them good enough to
stagger round a water well. You see, don't you, partner?
You see what I mean? You know, the men on the other
side—they get shiny new silver coins while we get only
lousy paper money printed in that murderer's factory,
that's what we get, yes, that's ours, I tell you!"

The majority of the soldiers spoke in much the same
tenor. Even a top sergeant candidly confessed, "Yes, I
enlisted all right. I wanted to. But, by God, I missed the
right side by a long shot. What you can't make in a life-
time, sweating like a mule and breaking your back in
peacetime, damn it all, you can make in a few months
just running around the sierra with a gun on your back,
but not with this crowd, dearie, not with this lousy
outfit. . . ."

Luis Cervantes, who already shared this hidden, im-
placably mortal hatred of the upper classes, of his officers, and of his superiors, felt that a veil had been removed from his eyes; clearly, now, he saw the final out-
come of the struggle. And yet what had happened? The
first moment he was able to join his coreligionists, instead of welcoming him with open arms, they threw him
into a pigsty with swine for company.

Day broke. The roosters crowed in the huts. The
chickens perched in the *huizache* began to stretch their
wings, shake their feathers, and fly down to the ground.

Luis Cervantes saw his guards lying on top of a dung
heap, snoring. In his imagination, he reviewed the features of last night's men. One, Pancracio, was pockmarked, blotchy, unshaven; his chin protruded, his

forehead receded obliquely; his ears formed one solid piece with head and neck—a horrible man. The other, Manteca, was so much human refuse; his eyes were almost hidden, his look sullen; his wiry straight hair fell over his ears, forehead and neck; his scrofulous lips hung eternally agape. Once more, Luis Cervantes felt his flesh quiver.

VII

STILL drowsy, Demetrio ran his hand through his ruffled hair, which hung over his moist forehead, pushed it back over his ears, and opened his eyes.

Distinctly he heard the woman's melodious voice which he had already sensed in his dream. He walked toward the door.

It was broad daylight; the rays of sunlight filtered through the thatch of the hut.

The girl who had offered him water the day before, the girl of whom he had dreamed all night long, now came forward, kindly and eager as ever. This time she carried a pitcher of milk brimming over with foam.

"It's goat's milk, but fine just the same. Come on now: taste it."

Demetrio smiled gratefully, straightened up, grasped the clay pitcher, and proceeded to drink the milk in little gulps, without removing his eyes from the girl.

She grew self-conscious, lowered her eyes.

"What's your name?" he asked.

"Camilla."

"Ah, there's a lovely name! And the girl that bears it, lovelier still!"

Camilla blushed. As he sought to seize her wrist, she grew frightened, and picking up the empty pitcher, flew out the door.

"No, Demetrio," Anastasio Montáñez commented gravely, "you've got to break them in first. Hmm! It's a hell of a lot of scars the women have left on my body. Yes, my friend, I've a heap of experience along that line."

"I feel all right now, Compadre." Demetrio pretended he had not heard him. "I had fever, and I sweated like a horse all night, but I feel quite fresh today. The thing

36

that's irking me hellishly is that Goddamn wound. Call Venancio to look after me."

"What are we going to do with the tenderfoot we caught last night?" Pancracio asked.

"That's right: I was forgetting all about him."

As usual, Demetrio hesitated a while before he reached a decision.

"Here, Quail, come here. Listen: you go and find out where's the nearest church around here. I know there's one about six miles away. Go and steal a priest's robe and bring it back."

"What's the idea?" asked Pancracio in surprise.

"Well, I'll soon find out if this tenderfoot came here to murder me. I'll tell him he's to be shot, see, and Quail will put on the priest's robes, say that he's a priest and hear his confession. If he's got anything up his sleeve, he'll come out with it, and then I'll shoot him. Otherwise I'll let him go."

"God, there's a roundabout way to tackle the question. If I were you, I'd just shoot him and let it go at that," said Pancracio contemptuously.

That night Quail returned with the priest's robes; Demetrio ordered the prisoner to be led in. Luis Cervantes had not eaten or slept for two days, there were deep black circles under his eyes; his face was deathly pale, his lips dry and colorless. He spoke awkwardly, slowly: "You can do as you please with me. . . . I am convinced I was wrong to come looking for you."

There was a prolonged silence. Then:

"I thought that you would welcome a man who comes to offer his help, with open arms, even though his help was quite worthless. After all, you might perhaps have found some use for it. What, in heaven's name, do I stand to gain, whether the revolution wins or loses?"

Little by little he grew more animated; at times the languor in his eyes disappeared.

"The revolution benefits the poor, the ignorant, all those who have been slaves all their lives, all the unhappy people who do not even suspect they are poor because the rich who stand above them, the rich who rule them, change their sweat and blood and tears into gold. . . ."

"Well, what the hell is the gist of all this palaver? I'll be damned if I can stomach a sermon," Pancracio broke in.

"I wanted to fight for the sacred cause of the oppressed, but you don't understand . . . you cast me aside. . . . Very well, then, you can do as you please with me!"

"All I'm going to do now is to put this rope around your neck. Look what a pretty white neck you've got."

"Yes, I know what brought you here," Demetrio interrupted dryly, scratching his head. "I'm going to have you shot!"

Then, looking at Anastasio, he said:

"Take him away. And . . . if he wants to confess, bring the priest to him."

Impassive as ever, Anastasio took the prisoner gently by the arm.

"Come along this way, Tenderfoot."

They all laughed uproariously, when a few minutes later, Quail appeared in priestly robes.

"By God, this tenderfoot certainly talks his head off," Quail said. "You know, I've a notion he was having a bit of a laugh on me when I started asking him questions."

"But didn't he have anything to say?"

"Nothing, save what he said last night."

"I've a hunch he didn't come here to shoot you at all, Compadre," said Anastasio.

"Give him something to eat and guard him."

VIII

ON the morrow, Luis Cervantes was barely able to get up. His injured leg trailing behind him, he shuffled from hut to hut in search of a little alcohol, a kettle of boiled water and some rags. With unfailing kindness, Camilla provided him with all that he wanted.

As he began washing his foot, she sat beside him, and, with typical mountaineer's curiosity, inquired:

"Tell me, who learned you how to cure people? Why did you boil that water? Why did you boil the rags? Look, look, how careful you are about everything! And what did you put on your hands? Really. . . . And why did you pour on alcohol? I just knew alcohol was good to rub on when you had a bellyache, but . . . Oh, I see! So you was going to be a doctor, huh? Ha, ha, that's a good one! Why don't you mix it with cold water! Well, there's a funny sort of a trick. Oh, stop fooling me . . . the idea: little animals alive in the water unless you boil it! Ugh! Well, I can't see nothing in it myself."

Camilla continued to cross-question him with such familiarity that she suddenly found herself addressing him intimately, in the singular *tu*. Absorbed in his own thoughts, Luis Cervantes had ceased listening to her. He thought:

Where are those men on Pancho Villa's payroll, so admirably equipped and mounted, who only get paid in those pure silver pieces Villa coins at the Chihuahua mint? Bah! Barely two dozen half-naked mangy men, some of them riding decrepit mares with the coat nibbled off from neck to withers. Can the accounts given by the Government newspapers and by myself be really true and are these so-called revolutionists simply bandits grouped together, using the revolution as a wonderful pretext to glut their thirst for gold and blood?

Is it all a lie, then? Were their sympathizers talking a lot of exalted nonsense?

If on one hand the Government newspapers vied with each other in noisy proclamation of Federal victory after victory, why then had a paymaster on his way from Guadalajara started the rumor that President Huerta's friends and relatives were abandoning the capital and scurrying away to the nearest port? Was Huerta's, "I shall have peace, at no matter what cost," a meaningless growl? Well, it looked as though the revolutionists or bandits, call them what you will, were going to depose the Government. Tomorrow would therefore belong wholly to them. A man must consequently be on their side, only on their side.

"No," he said to himself almost aloud, "I don't think I've made a mistake this time."

"What did you say?" Camilla asked. "I thought you'd lost your tongue. . . . I thought the mice had eaten it up!"

Luis Cervantes frowned and cast a hostile glance at this little plump monkey with her bronzed complexion, her ivory teeth, and her thick square toes.

"Look here, Tenderfoot, you know how to tell fairy stories, don't you?"

For all answer, Luis made an impatient gesture and moved off, the girl's ecstatic glance following his retreating figure until it was lost on the river path. So profound was her absorption that she shuddered in nervous surprise as she heard the voice of her neighbor, one-eyed María Antonia, who had been spying from her hut, shouting:

"Hey, you there: give him some love powder. Then he might fall for you."

"That's what you'd do, all right!"

"Oh, you think so, do you? Well, you're quite wrong! Faugh! I despise a tenderfoot, and don't forget it!"

IX

"HO there, Remigia, lend me some eggs, will you? My chicken has been hatching since morning. There's some gentlemen here, come to eat."

Her neighbor's eyes blinked as the bright sunlight poured into the shadowy hut, darker than usual, even, as dense clouds of smoke rose from the stove. After a few minutes, she began to make out the contour of the various objects inside, and recognized the wounded man's stretcher, which lay in one corner, close to the ashy-gray galvanized iron roof.

She sat down beside Remigia Indian-fashion, and, glancing furtively toward where Demetrio rested, asked in a low voice:

"How's the patient, better? That's fine. Oh, how young he is! But he's still pale, don't you think? So the wound's not closed up yet. Well, Remigia, don't you think we'd better try and do something about it?"

Remigia, naked from the waist up, stretched her thin muscular arms over the corn grinder, pounding the corn with a stone bar she held in her hands.

"Oh, I don't know; they might not like it," she answered, breathing heavily as she continued her rude task. "They've got their own doctor, you know, so—"

"Hallo, there, Remigia," another neighbor said as she came in, bowing her bony back to pass through the opening, "haven't you any laurel leaves? We want to make a potion for María Antonia who's not so well today, what with her bellyache."

In reality, her errand was but a pretext for asking questions and passing the time of day in gossip, so she turned her eyes to the corner where the patient lay and, winking, sought information as to his health.

Remigia lowered her eyes to indicate that Demetrio was sleeping.

"Oh, I didn't see you when I came in. And you're here too, Panchita? Well, how are you?"

"Good morning to you, Fortunata. How are *you?"*

"All right. But María Antonia's got the curse today and her belly's aching something fierce."

She sat Indian-fashion, with bent knees, huddling hip to hip against Panchita.

"I've got no laurel leaves, honey," Remigia answered, pausing a moment in her work to push a mop of hair back from over her sweaty forehead. Then, plunging her two hands into a mass of corn, she removed a handful of it dripping with muddy yellowish water. "I've none at all; you'd better go to Dolores, she's always got herbs, you know."

"But Dolores went to Cofradía last night. I don't know, but they say they came to fetch her to help Uncle Matías' girl who's big with child."

"You don't say, Panchita?"

The three old women came together forming an animated group, and speaking in low tones, began to gossip with great gusto.

"Certainly, I swear it, by God up there in heaven."

"Well, well, I was the first one to say that Marcelina was big with child, wasn't I? But of course no one would believe me."

"Poor girl. It's going to be terrible if the kid is her uncle's, you know!"

"God forbid!"

"Of course it's not her uncle: Nazario had nothing to do with it, *I* know. It was them damned soldiers, that's who done it."

"God, what a bloody mess! Another unhappy woman!"

The cackle of the old hens finally awakened Demetrio. They kept silent for a moment; then Panchita, taking out of the bosom of her blouse a young pigeon which opened its beak in suffocation, said:

"To tell you the truth, I brought this medicine for the gentleman here, but they say he's got a doctor, so I suppose—"

"That makes no difference, Panchita, that's no medicine anyhow, it's simply something to rub on his body."

"Forgive this poor gift from a poor woman, señor," said the wrinkled old woman, drawing close to Demetrio, "but there's nothing like it in the world for hemorrhages and suchlike."

Demetrio nodded hasty approval. They had already placed a loaf of bread soaked in alcohol on his stomach; although when this was removed he began to be cooler, he felt that he was still feverish inside.

"Come on, Remigia, you do it, you certainly know how," the women said.

Out of a reed sheath, Remigia pulled a long and curved knife which served to cut cactus fruit. She took the pigeon in one hand, turned it over, its breast upward, and with the skill of a surgeon, ripped it in two with a single thrust.

"In the name of Jesus, Mary, and Joseph," Remigia said, blessing the room and making the sign of the cross; next, with infinite dexterity, she placed the warm bleeding portions of the pigeon upon Demetrio's abdomen.

"You'll see: you'll feel much better now."

Obeying Remigia's instructions, Demetrio lay motionless, crumpled up on one side.

Then Fortunata gave vent to her sorrows. She liked these gentlemen of the revolution, all right, that she did —for, three months ago, you know, the Government soldiers had run away with her only daughter. This had broken her heart, yes, and driven her all but crazy.

As she began, Anastasio Montáñez and Quail lay on the floor near the stretcher, their mouths gaping, all ears to the story. But Fortunata's wealth of detail by the time she had told half of it bored Quail and he left the hut to scratch himself out in the sun. By the time Fortunata had at last concluded with a solemn "I pray God and the Blessed Virgin Mary that you are not sparing the life of a single one of those Federals from hell," Demetrio, face to wall, felt greatly relieved by the stomach cure, and was busy thinking of the best route by which to proceed to Durango. Anastasio Montáñez was snoring like a trombone.

X

"WHY don't you call in the tenderfoot to treat you, Compadre Demetrio," Anastasio Montáñez asked his chief, who had been complaining daily of chills and fever. "You ought to see him; no one has laid a hand to him but himself, and now he's so fit that he doesn't limp a step."

But Venancio, standing by with his tins of lard and his dirty string rags ready, protested:

"All right, if anybody lays a hand on Demetrio, I won't be responsible."

"Nonsense! Rot! What kind of doctor do you think you are? You're no doctor at all. I'll wager you've already forgotten why you ever joined us," said Quail.

"Well, I remember why you joined us, Quail," Venancio replied angrily. "Perhaps you'll deny it was because you had stolen a watch and some diamond rings."

"Ha, ha, ha! That's rich! But you're worse, my lad; you ran away from your hometown because you poisoned your sweetheart."

"You're a Goddamned liar!"

"Yes you did! And don't try and deny it! You fed her Spanish fly and . . ."

Venancio's shout of protest was drowned out in the loud laughter of the others. Demetrio, looking pale and sallow, motioned for silence. Then, plaintively:

"That'll do. Bring in the student."

Luis Cervantes entered. He uncovered Demetrio's wound, examined it carefully, and shook his head. The ligaments had made a furrow in the skin. The leg, badly swollen, seemed about to burst. At every move he made, Demetrio stifled a moan. Luis Cervantes cut the ligaments, soaked the wound in water, covered the leg with large clean rags and bound it up. Demetrio was able to

44

sleep all afternoon and all night. On the morrow he woke up happy.

"That tenderfoot has the softest hand in the world!" he said.

Quickly Venancio cut in:

"All right; just as you say. But don't forget that tenderfoots are like moisture, they seep in everywhere. It's the tenderfoots who stopped us reaping the harvest of the revolution."

Since Demetrio believed in the barber's knowledge implicitly, when Luis Cervantes came to treat him on the next day he said:

"Look here, do your best, see. I want to recover soon and then you can go home or anywhere else you damn well please."

Discreetly, Luis Cervantes made no reply.

A week, ten days, a fortnight elapsed. The Federal troops seemed to have vanished. There was an abundance of corn and beans, too, in the neighboring ranches. The people hated the Government so bitterly that they were overjoyed to furnish assistance to the rebels. Demetrio's men, therefore, were peacefully waiting for the complete recovery of their chief.

Day after day, Luis Cervantes remained humble and silent.

"By God, I actually believe you're in love," Demetrio said jokingly one morning after the daily treatment. He had begun to like this tenderfoot. From then on, Demetrio began gradually to show an increasing interest in Cervantes' comfort. One day he asked him if the soldiers gave him his daily ration of meat and milk; Luis Cervantes was forced to answer that his sole nourishment was whatever the old ranch women happened to give him and that everyone still considered him an intruder.

"Look here, Tenderfoot, they're all good boys, really," Demetrio answered. "You've got to know how to handle them, that's all. You mark my words; from tomorrow on, there won't be a thing you'll lack."

In effect, things began to change that very afternoon. Some of Demetrio's men lay in the quarry, glancing at the sunset that turned the clouds into huge clots of congealed blood and listening to Venancio's amusing stories culled from *The Wandering Jew*. Some of them, lulled by the narrator's mellifluous voice, began to snore. But Luis Cervantes listened avidly and as soon as Venancio topped off his talk with a storm of anticlerical denunciations he said emphatically: "Wonderful, wonderful! What intelligence! You're a most gifted man!"

"Well, I reckon it's not so bad," Venancio answered, warming to the flattery, "but my parents died and I didn't have a chance to study for a profession."

"That's easy to remedy, I'm sure. Once our cause is victorious, you can easily get a degree. A matter of two or three weeks' assistant's work at some hospital and a letter of recommendation from our chief and you'll be a full-fledged doctor, all right. The thing is child's play."

From that night onward Venancio, unlike the others, ceased calling him Tenderfoot. He addressed him as Louie.

It was Louie, this, and Louie, that, right and left, all the time.

XI

"Look here, Tenderfoot, I want to tell you something," Camilla called to Luis Cervantes, as he made his way to the hut to fetch some boiling water for his foot.

For days the girl had been restless. Her coy ways and her reticence had finally annoyed the man; stopping suddenly, he stood up and eyeing her squarely:

"All right. What do you want to tell me?"

Camilla's tongue clove to her mouth, heavy and damp as a rag; she could not utter a word. A blush suffused her cheeks, turning them red as apples; she shrugged her shoulders and bowed her head, pressing her chin against her naked breast. Then without moving, with the fixity of an idiot, she glanced at the wound, and said in a whisper:

"Look, how nicely it's healing now: it's like a red Castille rose."

Luis Cervantes frowned and with obvious disgust continued to care for his foot, completely ignoring her as he worked. When he had finished, Camilla had vanished.

For three days she was nowhere to be found. It was always her mother, Agapita, who answered Cervantes' call, and boiled the water for him and gave him rags. He was careful to avoid questioning her. Three days later, Camilla reappeared, more coy and eager than ever.

The more distrait and indifferent Luis Cervantes grew, the bolder Camilla. At last, she said: "Listen to me, you nice young fellow, I want to tell you something pleasant. Please go over the words of the revolutionary song 'Adelita' with me, will you? You can guess why, eh? I want to sing it and sing it, over again often and often, see? Then when you're off and away and when you've forgotten all about Camilla, it'll remind me of you."

To Luis Cervantes her words were like the noise of a

sharp steel knife drawn over the side of a glass bottle. Blissfully unaware of the effect they had produced, she proceeded, candid as ever:

"Well, I want to tell you something. You don't know that your chief is a wicked man, do you? Shall I tell you what he did to me? You know Demetrio won't let a soul but Mamma cook for him and me take him his food. Well, the other day I take some food over to him and what do you think he did to me, the old fool. He grabs hold of my wrist and he presses it tight, tight as can be, and then he starts pinching my legs.

" 'Come on, let me go,' I said. 'Keep still, lay off, you shameless creature. You've got no manners, that's the trouble with you.' So I wrestled with him, and shook myself free, like this, and ran off as fast as I could. What do you think of that?"

Camilla had never seen Luis Cervantes laugh so heartily.

"But it is really true, all this you've told me?"

Utterly at a loss, Camilla could not answer. Then he burst into laughter again and repeated the question. A sense of confusion came upon her. Disturbed, troubled, she said brokenly:

"Yes, it's the truth. And I wanted to tell you about it. But you don't seem to feel at all angry."

Once more Camilla glanced adoringly at Luis Cervantes' radiant, clean face; at his glaucous, soft eyes, his cheeks pink and polished as a porcelain doll's; at his tender white skin that showed below the line of his collar and on his shoulders, protruding from under a rough woolen poncho; at his hair, ever so slightly curled.

"What the devil are you waiting for, fool? If the chief likes you, what more do you want?"

Camilla felt something rise within her breast, an empty ache that became a knot when it reached her throat; she closed her eyes fast to hold back the tears that welled up in them. Then, with the back of her hand, she wiped her wet cheeks, and just as she had done three days ago, fled with all the swiftness of a young deer.

XII

DEMETRIO'S wound had already healed. They began to discuss various projects to go northward where, according to rumor, the rebels had beaten the Federal troops all along the line.

A certain incident came to precipitate their action. Seated on a crag of the sierra in the cool of the afternoon breeze, Luis Cervantes gazed away in the distance, dreaming and killing time. Below the narrow rock Pancracio and Manteca, lying like lizards between the *jarales* along one of the river margins, were playing cards. Anastasio Montáñez, looking on indifferently, turned his black hairy face toward Luis Cervantes and, leveling his kindly gaze upon him, asked:

"Why so sad, you from the city? What are you daydreaming about? Come on over here and let's have a chat!"

Luis Cervantes did not move; Anastasio went over to him and sat down beside him like a friend.

"What you need is the excitement of the city. I wager you shine your shoes every day and wear a necktie. Now, I may look dirty and my clothes may be torn to shreds, but I'm not really what I seem to be. I'm not here because I've got to be and don't you think so. Why, I own twenty oxen. Certainly I do; ask my friend Demetrio. I cleared ten bushels last harvest time. You see, if there's one thing I love, that's riling these Government fellows and making them furious. The last scrape I had—it'll be eight months gone now, ever since I've joined these men—I stuck my knife into some captain. He was just a nobody, a little Government squirt. I pinked him here, see, right under the navel. And that's why I'm here: that and because I wanted to give my mate Demetrio a hand."

"Christ! The bloody little darling of my life!" Manteca

shouted, waxing enthusiastic over a winning hand. He placed a twenty-cent silver coin on the jack of spades.

"If you want my opinion, I'm not much on gambling. Do you want to bet? Well, come on then, I'm game. How do you like the sound of this leather snake jingling, eh?"

Anastasio shook his belt; the silver coins rang as he shook them together.

Meanwhile, Pancracio dealt the cards, the jack of spades turned up out of the deck and a quarrel ensued. Altercation, noise, then shouts, and, at last, insults. Pancracio brought his stony face close to Manteca, who looked at him with snake's eyes, convulsive, foaming at the mouth. Another moment and they would have been exchanging blows. Having completely exhausted their stock of direct insults, they now resorted to the most flowery and ornate insulting of each other's ancestors, male and female, paternal or maternal. Yet nothing untoward occurred.

After their supply of words was exhausted, they gave over gambling and, their arms about each other's shoulders, marched off in search of a drink of alcohol.

"I don't like to fight with my tongue either, it's not decent. I'm right, too, eh? I tell you no man living has ever breathed a word to me against my mother. I want to be respected, see? That's why you've never seen me fooling with anyone." There was a pause. Then, suddenly, "Look there, Tenderfoot," Anastasio said, changing his tone and standing up with one hand spread over his eyes. "What's that dust over there behind the hillock. By God, what if it's those damned Federals and we sitting here doing nothing. Come on, let's go and warn the rest of the boys."

The news met with cries of joy.

"Ah, we're going to meet them!" cried Pancracio jubilantly, first among them to rejoice.

"Of course, we're going to meet them! We'll strip them clean of everything they brought with them."

A few moments later, amid cries of joy and a bustle of arms, they began saddling their horses. But the enemy turned out to be a few burros and two Indians, driving them forward.

"Stop them, anyhow. They must have come from some-where and they've probably news for us," Demetrio said.

Indeed, their news proved sensational. The Federal troops had fortified the hills in Zacatecas; this was said to be Huerta's last stronghold, but everybody predicted the fall of the city. Many families had hastily fled south-ward. Trains were overloaded with people; there was a scarcity of trucks and coaches; hundreds of people, panic-stricken, walked along the highroad with their be-longings in a pack slung over their shoulders. General Pánfilo Natera was assembling his men at Fresnillo; the Federals already felt it was all up with them.

"The fall of Zacatecas will be Huerta's *requiescat in pace*," Luis Cervantes cried with unusual excitement. "We've got to be there before the fight starts so that we can join Natera's army."

Then, suddenly, he noted the surprise with which De-metrio and his men greeted his suggestion. Crestfallen, he realized they still considered him of no account.

On the morrow, as the men set off in search of good mounts before taking to the road again, Demetrio called Luis Cervantes:

"Do you really want to come with us? Of course you're cut from another timber, we all know that; God knows why you should like this sort of life. Do you imagine we're in this game because we like it? Now, I like the ex-citement all right, but that's not all. Sit down here; that's right. Do you want to know why I'm a rebel? Well, I'll tell you.

"Before the revolution, I had my land all plowed, see, and just right for sowing and if it hadn't been for a little quarrel with Don Mónico, the boss of my town, Moya-hua, I'd be there in a jiffy getting the oxen ready for the sowing, see?

"Here, there, Pancracio, pull down two bottles of beer for me and this tenderfoot. . . . By the Holy Cross . . . drinking won't hurt me, now, will it?"

XIII

I WAS born in Limón, close by Moyahua, right in the heart of the Juchipila canyon. I had my house and my cows and a patch of land, see: I had everything I wanted. Well, I suppose you know how we farmers make a habit of going over to town every week to hear Mass and the sermon and then to market to buy our onions and tomatoes and in general everything they want us to buy at the ranch. Then you pick up some friends and go to Primitivo López' saloon for a bit of a drink before dinner; well, you sit there drinking and you've got to be sociable, so you drink more than you should and the liquor goes to your head and you laugh and you're damned happy and if you feel like it, you sing and shout and kick up a bit of a row. That's quite all right, anyhow, for we're not doing anyone any harm. But soon they start bothering you and the policeman walks up and down and stops occasionally, with his ear to the door. To put it in a nutshell, the chief of police and his gang are a lot of joykillers who decide they want to put a stop to your fun, see? But by God! You've got guts, you've got red blood in your veins and you've got a soul, too, see? So you lose your temper, you stand up to them and tell them to go to the Devil.

"Now if they understand you, everything's all right; they leave you alone and that's all there is to it; but sometimes they try to talk you down and hit you and—well, you know how it is, a fellow's quick-tempered and he'll be damned if he'll stand for someone ordering him around and telling him what's what. So before you know it, you've got your knife out or your gun leveled, and then off you go for a wild run in the sierra, until they've forgotten the corpse, see?

"All right: that's just about what happened to Mónico. The fellow was a greater bluffer than the rest. He couldn't tell a rooster from a hen, not he. Well, I spit on his beard because he wouldn't mind his own business. That's all, there's nothing else to tell.

"Then, just because I did that, he had the whole God-damned Federal Government against me. You must have heard something about that story in Mexico City—about the killing of Madero and some 'other fellow, Félix or Felipe Díaz, or something—I don't know. Well, this man Mónico goes in person to Zacatecas to get an army to capture me. They said that I was a Maderista and that I was going to rebel. But a man like me always has friends. Somebody came and warned me of what was coming to me, so when the soldiers reached Limón I was miles and miles away. Trust me! Then my compadre Anastasio who killed somebody came and joined me, and Pancracio and Quail and a lot of friends and acquaintances came after him. Since then we've been sort of collecting, see? You know for yourself, we get along as best we can. . . ."

For a while, both men sat meditating in silence. Then:

"Look here, Chief," said Luis Cervantes. "You know that some of Natera's men are at Juchipila, quite near here. I think we should join them before they capture Zacatecas. All we need do is speak to the General."

"I'm no good at that sort of thing. And I don't like the idea of accepting orders from anybody very much."

"But you've only a handful of men down here; you'll only be an unimportant chieftain. There's no argument about it, the revolution is bound to win. After it's all over they'll talk to you just as Madero talked to all those who had helped him: 'Thank you very much, my friends, you can go home now. . . .'"

"Well that's all I want, to be let alone so I can go home."

"Wait a moment, I haven't finished. Madero said: 'You men have made me President of the Republic. You have run the risk of losing your lives and leaving your wives and children destitute; now I have what I wanted, you can go back to your picks and shovels, you can resume your hand-to-mouth existence, you can go half-naked and hungry just as you did before, while we, your superiors, will go about trying to pile up a few million pesos. . . .' "

Demetrio nodded and, smiling, scratched his head.

"You said a mouthful, Louie," Venancio the barber put in enthusiastically. "A mouthful as big as a church!"

"As I was saying," Luis Cervantes resumed, "when the revolution is over, everything is over. Too bad that so many men have been killed, too bad there are so many widows and orphans, too bad there was so much bloodshed.

"Of course, you are not selfish; you say to yourself: 'All I want to do is go back home.' But I ask you, is it fair to deprive your wife and kids of a fortune which God himself places within reach of your hand? Is it fair to abandon your motherland in this solemn moment when she most needs the self-sacrifice of her sons, when she most needs her humble sons to save her from falling again in the clutches of her eternal oppressors, executioners, and *caciques?* You must not forget that the thing a man holds most sacred on earth is his motherland."

Macías smiled, his eyes shining.

"Will it be all right if we go with Natera?"

"Not only all right," Venancio said insinuatingly, "but I think it absolutely necessary."

"Now Chief," Cervantes pursued, "I took a fancy to you the first time I laid eyes on you and I like you more and more every day because I realize what you are worth. Please let me be utterly frank. You do not yet realize your lofty noble function. You are a modest man without ambitions, you do not wish to realize the exceedingly important role you are destined to play in the revolution. It is not true that you took up arms simply because of Señor Mónico. You are under arms to protest against the evils of all the *caciques* who are overrunning the whole nation. We are the elements of a social movement which will not rest until it has enlarged the destinies of our motherland. We are the tools Destiny makes use of to reclaim the sacred rights of the people. We are not fighting to dethrone a miserable murderer, we are fighting against tyranny itself. What moves us is what men call ideals; our action is what men call fighting for a principle. A principle! That's why Villa and Natera and Carranza are fighting; that's why we, every man of us, are fighting."

"Yes . . . yes . . . exactly what I've been thinking myself," said Venancio in a climax of enthusiasm.

"Hey, there, Pancracio," Macías called, "pull down two more beers."

XIV

YOU ought to see how clear that fellow can make things, Compadre," Demetrio said. All morning long he had been pondering as much of Luis Cervantes' speech as he had understood.

"I heard him too," Anastasio answered. "People who can read and write get things clear, all right; nothing was ever truer. But what I can't make out is how you're going to go and meet Natera with as few men as we have."

"That's nothing. We're going to do things different now. They tell me that as soon as Crispín Robles enters a town he gets hold of all the horses and guns in the place; then he goes to the jail and lets all the jailbirds out, and, before you know it, he's got plenty of men, all right. You'll see. You know I'm beginning to feel that we haven't done things right so far. It don't seem right somehow that this city guy should be able to tell us what to do."

"Ain't it wonderful to be able to read and write!"

They both sighed, sadly. Luis Cervantes came in with several others to find out the day of their departure.

"We're leaving no later than tomorrow," said Demetrio without hesitation.

Quail suggested that musicians be summoned from the neighboring hamlet and that a farewell dance be given. His idea met with enthusiasm on all sides.

"We'll go, then," Pancracio shouted, "but I'm certainly going in good company this time. My sweetheart's coming along with me!"

Demetrio replied that he too would willingly take along a girl he had set his eye on, but that he hoped none of his men would leave bitter memories behind them as the Federals did.

"You won't have long to wait. Everything will be arranged when you return," Luis Cervantes whispered to him.

"What do you mean?" Demetrio asked. "I thought that you and Camilla . . ."

"There's not a word of truth in it, Chief. She likes you but she's afraid of you, that's all."

"Really? Is that really true?"

"Yes. But I think you're quite right in not wanting to leave any bitter feelings behind you as you go. When you come back as a conqueror, everything will be different. They'll all thank you for it even."

"By God, you're certainly a shrewd one," Demetrio replied, patting him on the back.

At sundown, Camilla went to the river to fetch water as usual. Luis Cervantes, walking down the same trail, met her. Camilla felt her heart leap to her mouth. But, without taking the slightest notice of her, Luis Cervantes hastily took one of the turns and disappeared among the rocks.

At this hour, as usual, the calcinated rocks, the sunburnt branches, and the dry weeds faded into the semiobscurity of the shadows. The wind blew softly, the green lances of the young corn leaves rustling in the twilight. Nothing was changed; all nature was as she had found it before, evening upon evening; but in the stones and the dry weeds, amid the fragrance of the air and the light whir of falling leaves, Camilla sensed a new strangeness, a vast desolation in everything about her.

Rounding a huge eroded rock, suddenly Camilla found herself face to face with Luis, who was seated on a stone, hatless, his legs dangling.

"Listen, you might come down here to say good-bye."

Luis Cervantes was obliging enough; he jumped down and joined her.

"You're proud, ain't you? Have I been so mean that you don't even want to talk to me?"

"Why do you say that, Camilla? You've been extremely kind to me; why, you've been more than a friend, you've taken care of me as if you were my sister. Now I'm about to leave, I'm very grateful to you; I'll always remember you."

"Liar!" Camilla said, her face transfigured with joy. "Suppose I hadn't come after you?"

"I intended to say good-bye to you at the dance this evening."

"What dance? If there's a dance, I'll not go to it."

"Why not?"

"Because I can't stand that horrible man . . . Demetrio!"

"Don't be silly, child," said Luis. "He's really very fond of you. Don't go and throw away this opportunity. You'll never have one like it again in your life. Don't you know that Demetrio is on the point of becoming a general, you silly girl? He'll be a very wealthy man, with horses galore; and you'll have jewels and clothes and a fine house and a lot of money to spend. Just imagine what a life you would lead with him!"

Camilla stared up at the blue sky so he should not read the expression in her eyes. A dead leaf shook slowly loose from the crest of a tree swinging slowly on the wind, fell like a small dead butterfly at her feet. She bent down and took it in her fingers. Then, without looking at him, she murmured:

"It's horrible to hear you talk like that. . . . I like you . . . no one else. . . . Ah, well, go then, go: I feel ashamed now. Please leave me!"

She threw away the leaf she had crumpled in her hand and covered her face with a corner of her apron. When she opened her eyes, Luis Cervantes had disappeared.

She followed the river trail. The river seemed to have been sprinkled with a fine red dust. On its surface drifted now a sky of variegated colors, now the dark crags, half light, half shadow. Myriads of luminous insects twinkled in a hollow. Camilla, standing on the beach of washed, round stones, caught a reflection of herself in the waters; she saw herself in her yellow blouse with the green ribbons, her white skirt, her carefully combed hair, her wide eyebrows and broad forehead, exactly as she had dressed to please Luis. She burst into tears.

Among the reeds, the frogs chanted the implacable melancholy of the hour. Perched on a dry root, a dove wept also.

XV

THAT evening, there was much merrymaking at the dance, and a great quantity of *mezcal* was drunk.

"I miss Camilla," said Demetrio in a loud voice.

Everybody looked about for Camilla.

"She's sick, she's got a headache," said Agapita harshly, uneasy as she caught sight of the malicious glances leveled at her.

When the dance was over, Demetrio, somewhat unsteady on his feet, thanked all the kind neighbors who had welcomed them and promised that when the revolution had triumphed he would remember them one and all, because "hospital or jail is a true test of friendship."

"May God's hand lead you all," said an old woman.

"God bless you all and keep you well," others added.

Utterly drunk, María Antonia said:

"Come back soon, damn soon!"

On the morrow, María Antonia, who, though she was pockmarked and walleyed, nevertheless enjoyed a notorious reputation—indeed it was confidently proclaimed that no man had failed to go with her behind the river weeds at some time or other—shouted to Camilla:

"Hey there, you! What's the matter? What are you doing there skulking in the corner with a shawl tied round your head! You're crying, I wager. Look at her eyes; they look like a witch's. There's no sorrow lasts more than three days!"

Agapita knitted her eyebrows and muttered indistinctly to herself.

The old crones felt uneasy and lonesome since Demetrio's men had left. The men, too, in spite of their gossip and insults, lamented their departure since now they would have no one to bring them fresh meat every day.

It is pleasant indeed to spend your time eating and drinking, and sleeping all day long in the cool shade of the rocks, while clouds ravel and unravel their fleecy threads on the blue shuttle of the sky.

"Look at them again. There they go!" María Antonia yelled. "Why, they look like toys."

Demetrio's men, riding their thin nags, could still be descried in the distance against the sapphire translucence of the sky, where the broken rocks and the chaparral melted into a single bluish smooth surface. Across the air a gust of hot wind bore the broken, faltering strains of "La Adelita," the revolutionary song, to the settlement. Camilla, who had come out when María Antonia shouted, could no longer control herself; she dived back into her hut, unable to restrain her tears and moaning. María Antonia burst into laughter and moved off.

"They've cast the evil eye on my daughter," Agapita said in perplexity. She pondered a while, then duly reached a decision. From a pole in the hut she took down a piece of strong leather which her husband used to hitch up the yoke. This pole stood between a picture of Christ and one of the Virgin. Agapita promptly twisted the leather and proceeded to administer a sound thrashing to Camilla in order to dispel the evil spirits.

Riding proudly on his horse, Demetrio felt like a new man. His eyes recovered their peculiar metallic brilliance, and the blood flowed, red and warm, through his coppery, pure-blooded Aztec cheeks.

The men threw out their chests as if to breathe the widening horizon, the immensity of the sky, the blue from the mountains and the fresh air, redolent with the various odors of the sierra. They spurred their horses to a gallop as if in that mad race they laid claims of possession to the earth. What man among them now remembered the stern chief of police, the growling policeman, or the conceited *cacique*? What man remembered his pitiful hut where he slaved away, always under the eyes of the owner or the ruthless and sullen foreman, always forced to rise before dawn, and to take up his shovel, basket, or goad, wearing himself out to earn a mere pitcher of *atole* and a handful of beans?

They laughed, they sang, they whistled, drunk with the sunlight, the air of the open spaces, the wine of life.

Meco, prancing forward on his horse, bared his white glistening teeth, joking and kicking up like a clown.

"Hey, Pancracio," he asked with utmost seriousness, "my wife writes me I've got another kid. How in hell is that? I ain't seen her since Madero was President."

"That's nothing," the other replied. "You just left her a lot of eggs to hatch for you!"

They all laughed uproariously. Only Meco, grave and aloof, sang in a voice horribly shrill:

> *"I gave her a penny*
> *That wasn't enough.*
> *I gave her a nickel*
> *The wench wanted more.*
> *We bargained. I asked*
> *If a dime was enough*
> *But she wanted a quarter.*
> *By God! That was tough!*
> *All wenches are fickle*
> *And trumpery stuff!"*

The sun, beating down upon them, dulled their minds and bodies and presently they were silent. All day long they rode through the canyon, up and down the steep, round hills, dirty and bald as a man's head, hill after hill in endless succession. At last, late in the afternoon, they descried several stone church towers in the heart of a bluish ridge, and, beyond, the white road with its curling spirals of dust and its gray telegraph poles.

They advanced toward the main road; in the distance they spied a figure of an Indian sitting on the embankment. They drew up to him. He proved to be an unfriendly looking old man, clad in rags; he was laboriously attempting to mend his leather sandals with the help of a dull knife. A burro loaded with fresh green grass stood by. Demetrio accosted him.

"What are you doing, Grandpa?"

"Gathering alfalfa for my cow."

"How many Federals are there around here?"

"Just a few: not more than a dozen, I reckon."

The old man grew communicative. He told them of many important rumors: Obregón was besieging Guadalajara, Torres was in complete control of the Potosí region, Natera ruled over Fresnillo.

"All right," said Demetrio, "you can go where you're headed for, see, but you be damn careful not to tell anyone you saw us, because if you do, I'll pump you full of lead. And I could track you down, even if you tried to hide in the pit of hell, see?"

"What do you say, boys?" Demetrio asked them as soon as the old man had disappeared.

"To hell with the *mochos!* We'll kill every blasted one of them!" they cried in unison.

Then they set to counting their cartridges and the hand grenades the Owl had made out of fragments of iron tubing and metal bed handles.

"Not much to brag about, but we'll soon trade them for rifles," Anastasio observed.

Anxiously they pressed forward, spurring the thin flanks of their nags to a gallop. Demetrio's brisk, imperious tones of order brought them abruptly to a halt.

They dismounted by the side of a hill, protected by thick *huizache* trees. Without unsaddling their horses, each began to search for stones to serve as pillows.

XVI

At midnight Demetrio Macías ordered the march to be resumed. The town was five or six miles away; the best plan was to take the soldiers by surprise, before reveille.

The sky was cloudy, with here and there a star shining. From time to time a flash of lightning crossed the sky with a red dart, illumining the far horizon.

Luis Cervantes asked Demetrio whether the success of the attack might not be better served by procuring a guide or leastways by ascertaining the topographic conditions of the town and the precise location of the soldiers' quarters.

"No," Demetrio answered, accompanying his smile with a disdainful gesture, "we'll simply fall on them when they least expect it; that's all there is to it, see? We've done it before all right, lots of times! Haven't you ever seen the squirrels stick their heads out of their holes when you poured in water? Well, that's how these lousy soldiers are going to feel. Do you see? They'll be frightened out of their wits the moment they hear our first shot. Then they'll slink out and stand as targets for us."

"Suppose the old man we met yesterday lied to us. Suppose there are fifty soldiers instead of twenty. Who knows but he's a spy sent out by the Federals!"

"Ha, Tenderfoot, frightened already, eh?" Anastasio Montáñez mocked.

"Sure! Handling a rifle and messing about with bandages are two different things," Pancracio observed.

"Well, that's enough talk, I guess," said Meco. "All we have to do is fight a dozen frightened rats."

"This fight won't convince our mothers that they gave birth to men or whatever the hell you like. . . ." Manteca added.

When they reached the outskirts of the town, Venancio walked ahead and knocked at the door of a hut.

64

"Where's the soldiers' barracks?" he inquired of a man who came out barefoot, a ragged serape covering his body.

"Right there, just beyond the Plaza," he answered.

Since nobody knew where the city square was, Venancio made him walk ahead to show the way. Trembling with fear, the poor devil told them they were doing him a terrible wrong.

"I'm just a poor day laborer, sir; I've got a wife and a lot of kids."

"What the hell do you think I have, dogs?" Demetrio scowled. "I've got kids too, see?"

Then he commanded:

"You men keep quiet. Not a sound out of you! And walk down the middle of the street, single file."

The rectangular church cupola rose above the small houses.

"Here, gentlemen; there's the Plaza beyond the church. Just walk a bit further and there's the barracks."

He knelt down, then, imploring them to let him go, but Pancracio, without pausing to reply, struck him across the chest with his rifle and ordered him to proceed.

"How many soldiers are there?" Luis Cervantes asked.

"I don't want to lie to you, boss, but to tell you the truth, yes, sir, to tell you God's truth, there's a lot of them, a whole lot of 'em."

Luis Cervantes turned around to stare at Demetrio, who feigned momentary deafness.

They were soon in the city square.

A loud volley of rifle shots rang out, deafening them. Demetrio's horse reared, staggered on its hind legs, bent its forelegs, and fell to the ground, kicking. The Owl uttered a piercing cry and fell from his horse which rushed madly to the center of the square.

Another volley: the guide threw up his arms and fell on his back without a sound.

With all haste, Anastasio Montáñez helped Demetrio up behind him on his horse; the others retreated, seeking shelter along the walls of the houses.

"Hey, men," said a workman sticking his head out of a large door, "go for 'em through the back of the chapel. They're all in there. Cut back through this street, then turn to the left; you'll reach an alley. Keep on going ahead until you hit the chapel."

As he spoke a fresh volley of pistol shots, directed from the neighboring roofs, fell like a rain about them.

"By God," the man said, "those ain't poisonous spiders; they're only townsmen scared of their own shadow. Come in here until they stop."

"How many of them are there?" asked Demetrio.

"There were only twelve of them. But last night they were scared out of their wits so they wired to the town beyond for help. I don't know how many of them there are now. Even if there are a hell of a lot of them, it doesn't cut any ice! Most of them aren't soldiers, you know, but drafted men; if just one of them starts mutinying, the rest will follow like sheep. My brother was drafted; they've got him there. I'll go along with you and signal to him; all of them will desert and follow you. Then we'll only have the officers to deal with! If you want to give me a gun or something. . . ."

"No more rifles left, brother. But I guess you can put these to some use," Anastasio Montáñez said, passing him two hand grenades.

The officer in command of the Federals was a young coxcomb of a captain with a waxed mustache and blond hair. As long as he felt uncertain about the strength of the assailants, he had remained extremely quiet and prudent; but now that they had driven the rebels back without allowing them a chance to fire a single shot, he waxed bold and brave. While the soldiers did not dare put out their heads beyond the pillars of the building, his own shadow stood against the pale clear dawn, exhibiting his well-built slender body and his officer's cape bellying in the breeze.

"Ha, I remember our *coup d'état!*"

His military career had consisted of the single adventure when, together with other students of the Officers' School, he was involved in the treacherous revolt of Féliz Díaz and Huerta against President Madero. Whenever the slightest insubordination arose, he invariably recalled his feat at the *Ciudadela.*

"Lieutenant Campos," he ordered emphatically, "take a dozen men and wipe out the bandits hiding there! The curs! They're only brave when it comes to guzzling meat and robbing a hencoop!"

A workingman appeared at the small door of the spiral staircase, announcing that the assailants were hidden in a corral where they might easily be captured. This message came from the citizens keeping watch on housetops.

"I'll go myself and get it over with!" the officer declared impetuously.

But he soon changed his mind. Before he had reached the door, he retraced his steps.

"Very likely they are waiting for more men and, of course, it would be wrong for me to abandon my post. Lieutenant Campos, go there yourself and capture them dead or alive. We'll shoot them at noon when everybody's coming out of church. Those bandits will see the example I'll set around here. But if you can't capture them, Lieutenant, kill them all. Don't leave a man of them alive, do you understand?"

In high good humor, he began pacing up and down the room, formulating the official despatch he would send off no later than today.

To His Honor the Minister for War,
General A. Blanquet,
Mexico City.

Sir:

I have the honor to inform your Excellency that on the morning of . . . a rebel army, five hundred strong, commanded by . . . attacked this town, which I am charged to defend. With such speed as the gravity of the situation called for, I fortified my post in the town. The battle lasted two hours. Despite the superiority of the enemy in men and equipment, I was able to defeat and rout them. Their casualties were twenty killed and a far greater number of wounded, judging from the trails of blood they left behind them as they retreated. I am pleased to state there was no casualty on our side. I have the honor to congratulate Your Excellency upon this new triumph for the Federal arms. Viva Presidente Huerta! Viva México!

"Well," the young captain mused, "I'll be promoted to major." He clasped his hands together, jubilant. At this precise moment, a detonation rang out. His ears buzzed, he—

XVII

IF we get through the corral, we can make the alley, eh?" Demetrio asked.

"That's right," the workman answered. "Beyond the corral there's a house, then another corral, then there's a store."

Demetrio scratched his head, thoughtfully. This time his decision was immediate.

"Can you get hold of a crowbar or something like that to make a hole through the wall?"

"Yes, we'll get anything you want, but . . ."

"But what? Where can we get a crowbar?"

"Everything is right there. But it all belongs to the boss."

Without further ado, Demetrio strode into the shed which had been pointed out as the toolhouse.

It was all a matter of a few minutes. Once in the alley, hugging to the walls, they marched forward in single file until they reached the rear of the church. Now they had but a single fence and the rear wall of the chapel to scale.

"God's will be done!" Demetrio said to himself. He was the first to clamber over.

Like monkeys the others followed him, reaching the other side with bleeding, grimy hands. The rest was easy. The deep worn steps along the stonework made their ascent of the chapel wall swifter. The church vault hid them from the soldiers.

"Wait a moment, will you?" said the workman. "I'll go and see where my brother is; I'll let you know and then you'll get at the officers."

But no one paid the slightest attention to him.

For a second, Demetrio glanced at the soldiers' black coats hanging on the wall, then at his own men, thick on the church tower behind the iron rail. He smiled with satisfaction and turning to his men said:

"Come on, now, boys!"

Twenty bombs exploded simultaneously in the midst of the soldiers who, awaking terrified out of their sleep, started up, their eyes wide open. But before they had realized their plight, twenty more bombs burst like thunder upon them leaving a scattering of men killed or maimed.

"Don't do that yet, for God's sake! Don't do it till I find my brother," the workman implored in anguish.

In vain an old sergeant harangued the soldiers, insulting them in the hope of rallying them. For they were rats, caught in a trap, no more, no less. Some of the soldiers, attempting to reach the small door by the staircase, fell to the ground pierced by Demetrio's shots. Others fell at the feet of these twenty-odd specters, with faces and breasts dark as iron, clad in long torn trousers of white cloth which fell to their leather sandals, scattering death and destruction below them. In the belfry, a few men struggled to emerge from the pile of dead who had fallen upon them.

"It's awful, Chief!" Luis Cervantes cried in alarm. "We've no more bombs left and we left our guns in the corral."

Smiling, Demetrio drew out a large shining knife. In the twinkling of an eye, steel flashed in every hand. Some knives were large and pointed, others wide as the palm of a hand, others heavy as bayonets.

"The spy!" Luis Cervantes cried triumphantly. "Didn't I tell you?"

"Don't kill me, Chief, please don't kill me," the old sergeant implored squirming at the feet of Demetrio, who stood over him, knife in hand. The victim raised his wrinkled Indian face; there was not a single gray hair in his head today. Demetrio recognized the spy who had lied to him the day before. Terrified, Luis Cervantes quickly averted his face. The steel blade went *crack, crack,* on the old man's ribs. He toppled backward, his arms spread, his eyes ghastly.

"Don't kill my brother, don't kill him, he's my brother!" the workman shouted in terror to Pancracio who was pursuing a soldier. But it was too late. With one thrust,

Pancracio had cut his neck in half, and two streams of scarlet spurted from the wound.

"Kill the soldiers, kill them all!"

Pancracio and Manteca surpassed the others in the savagery of their slaughter, and finished up with the wounded. Montáñez, exhausted, let his arm fall; it hung limp to his side. A gentle expression still filled his glance; his eyes shone; he was naïve as a child, unmoral as a hyena.

"Here's one who's not dead yet," Quail shouted.

Pancracio ran up. The little blond captain with curled mustache turned pale as wax. He stood against the door to the staircase unable to muster enough strength to take another step.

Pancracio pushed him brutally to the edge of the corridor. A jab with his knee against the captain's thigh—then a sound not unlike a bag of stones falling from the top of the steeple on the porch of the church.

"My God, you've got no brains!" said Quail. "If I'd known what you were doing, I'd have kept him for myself. That was a fine pair of shoes you lost!"

Bending over them, the rebels stripped those among the soldiers who were best clad, laughing and joking as they despoiled them. Brushing back his long hair, that had fallen over his sweating forehead and covered his eyes, Demetrio said:

"Now let's get those city fellows!"

XVIII

ON the day General Natera began his advance against the town of Zacatecas, Demetrio with a hundred men went to meet him at Fresnillo.

The leader received him cordially.

"I know who you are and the sort of men you bring. I heard about the beatings you gave the Federals from Tepic to Durango."

Natera shook hands with Demetrio effusively while Luis Cervantes said:

"With men like General Natera and Colonel Demetrio Macías, we'll cover our country with glory."

Demetrio understood the purpose of those words, after Natera had repeatedly addressed him as "Colonel."

Wine and beer were served; Demetrio and Natera drank many a toast. Luis Cervantes proposed: "The triumph of our cause, which is the sublime triumph of Justice, because our ideal—to free the noble, long-suffering people of Mexico—is about to be realized and because those men who have watered the earth with their blood and tears will reap the harvest which is rightfully theirs."

Natera fixed his cruel gaze on the orator, then turned his back on him to talk to Demetrio. Presently, one of Natera's officers, a young man with a frank open face, drew up to the table and stared insistently at Cervantes.

"Are you Luis Cervantes?"

"Yes. You're Solís, eh?"

"The moment you entered I thought I recognized you. Well, well, even now I can hardly believe my eyes!"

"It's true though!"

"Well, but . . . look here, let's have a drink, come along." Then:

71

"Hm," Solís went on, offering Cervantes a chair, "since when have you turned rebel?"

"I've been a rebel the last two months!"

"Oh, I see! That's why you speak with such faith and enthusiasm about things we all felt when we joined the revolution."

"Have you lost your faith or enthusiasm?"

"Look here, man, don't be surprised if I confide in you right off. I am so anxious to find someone intelligent among this crowd, that as soon as I get hold of a man like you I clutch at him as eagerly as I would at a glass of water, after walking mile after mile through a parched desert. But frankly, I think you should do the explaining first. I can't understand how a man who was correspondent of a Government newspaper during the Madero regime, and later editorial writer on a Conservative journal, who denounced us as bandits in the most fiery articles, is now fighting on our side."

"I tell you honestly: I have been converted," Cervantes answered.

"Are you absolutely convinced?"

Solís sighed, filled the glasses; they drank.

"What about you? Are you tired of the revolution?" asked Cervantes sharply.

"Tired? My dear fellow, I'm twenty-five years old and I'm fit as a fiddle! But am I disappointed? Perhaps!"

"You must have sound reasons for feeling that way."

"I hoped to find a meadow at the end of the road, I found a swamp. Facts are bitter; so are men. That bitterness eats your heart out; it is poison, dry rot. Enthusiasm, hope, ideals, happiness—vain dreams, vain dreams. . . . When that's over, you have a choice. Either you turn bandit, like the rest, or the timeservers will swamp you. . . ."

Cervantes writhed at his friend's words; his argument was quite out of place . . . painful. . . . To avoid being forced to take issue, he invited Solís to cite the circumstances that had destroyed his illusions.

"Circumstances? No—it's far less important than that. It's a host of silly, insignificant things that no one notices except yourself . . . a change of expression, eyes shining—lips curled in a sneer—the deep import of a phrase that is lost! Yet take these things together and they compose the mask of our race . . . terrible . . . grotesque . . . a race that awaits redemption!"

He drained another glass. After a long pause, he continued:

"You ask me why I am still a rebel? Well, the revolution is like a hurricane: if you're in it, you're not a man . . . you're a leaf, a dead leaf, blown by the wind."

Demetrio reappeared. Seeing him, Solís relapsed into silence.

"Come along," Demetrio said to Cervantes. "Come with me."

Unctuously, Solís congratulated Demetrio on the feats that had won him fame and the notice of Pancho Villa's northern division.

Demetrio warmed to his praise. Gratefully, he heard his prowess vaunted, though at times he found it difficult to believe he was the hero of the exploits the other narrated. But Solís' story proved so charming, so convincing, that before long he found himself repeating it as gospel truth.

"Natera is a genius!" Luis Cervantes said when they had returned to the hotel. "But Captain Solís is a nobody . . . a timeserver."

Demetrio Macías was too elated to listen to him.

"I'm a colonel, my lad! And you're my secretary!"

Demetrio's men made many acquaintances that evening; much liquor flowed to celebrate new friendships. Of course men are not necessarily even tempered, nor is alcohol a good counselor; quarrels naturally ensued. Yet many differences that occurred were smoothed out in a friendly spirit, outside the saloons, restaurants, or brothels.

On the morrow, casualties were reported. Always a few dead. An old prostitute was found with a bullet through her stomach; two of Colonel Macías' new men lay in the gutter, slit from ear to ear.

Anastasio Montáñez carried an account of the events to his chief. Demetrio shrugged his shoulders.

"Bury them!" he said.

XIX

"THEY'RE coming back!"

It was with amazement that the inhabitants of Fresnillo learned that the rebel attack on Zacatecas had failed completely.

"They're coming back!"

The rebels were a maddened mob, sunburnt, filthy, naked. Their high wide-brimmed straw hats hid their faces. The "high hats" came back as happily as they had marched forth a few days before, pillaging every hamlet along the road, every ranch, even the poorest hut.

"Who'll buy this thing?" one of them asked. He had carried his spoils long: he was tired. The sheen of the nickel on the typewriter, a new machine, attracted every glance. Five times that morning the Oliver had changed hands. The first sale netted the owner ten pesos; presently it had sold for eight; each time it changed hands, it was two pesos cheaper. To be sure, it was a heavy burden; nobody could carry it for more than a half-hour.

"I'll give you a quarter for it!" Quail said.

"Yours!" cried the owner, handing it over quickly, as though he feared Quail might change his mind. Thus for the sum of twenty-five cents, Quail was afforded the pleasure of taking it in his hands and throwing it with all his might against the wall.

It struck with a crash. This gave the signal to all who carried any cumbersome objects to get rid of them by smashing them against the rocks. Objects of all sorts, crystal, china, faïence, porcelain, flew through the air. Heavy, plated mirrors, brass candlesticks, fragile, delicate statues, Chinese vases, any object not readily convertible into cash fell by the wayside in fragments.

Demetrio did not share the untoward exaltation. After

74

all, they were retreating defeated. He called Montáñez and Pancracio aside and said:

"These fellows have no guts. It's not so hard to take a town. It's like this. First, you open up, this way. . . ." He sketched a vast gesture, spreading his powerful arms. "Then you get close to them, like this. . . ." He brought his arms together, slowly. "Then slam! Bang! Whack! Crash!" He beat his hands against his chest.

Anastasio and Pancracio, convinced by this simple, lucid explanation answered:

"That's God's truth! They've no guts! That's the trouble with them!"

Demetrio's men camped in a corral.

"Do you remember Camilla?" Demetrio asked with a sigh as he settled on his back on the manure pile where the rest were already stretched out.

"Camilla? What girl do you mean, Demetrio?"

"The girl that used to feed me up there at the ranch!"

Anastasio made a gesture implying: "I don't care a damn about the women . . . Camilla or anyone else. . . ."

"I've not forgotten," Demetrio went on, drawing on his cigarette. "Yes, I was feeling like hell! I'd just finished drinking a glass of water. God, but it was cool. . . . 'Don't you want any more?' she asked me. I was half dead with fever . . . and all the time I saw that glass of water, blue . . . so blue . . . and I heard her little voice, 'Don't you want any more?' That voice tinkled in my ears like a silver hurdy-gurdy! Well, Pancracio, what about it? Shall we go back to the ranch?"

"Demetrio, we're friends, aren't we? Well then, listen. You may not believe it, but I've had a lot of experience with women. Women! Christ, they're all right for a while, granted! Though even that's going pretty far. Demetrio, you should see the scars they've given me . . . all over my body, not to speak of my soul! To hell with women. They're the devil, that's what they are! You may have noticed I steer clear of them. You know why. And don't think I don't know what I'm talking about. I've had a hell of a lot of experience and that's no lie!"

"What do you say, Pancracio? When are we going back to the ranch?" Demetrio insisted, blowing gray clouds of tobacco smoke into the air.

"Say the day, I'm game. You know I left my woman there too!"

"Your woman, hell!" Quail said, disgruntled and sleepy.

"All right, then, our woman! It's a good thing you're kindhearted so we all can enjoy her when you bring her over," Manteca murmured.

"That's right, Pancracio, bring one-eyed María Antonia. We're all getting pretty cold around here," Meco shouted from a distance.

The crowd broke into peals of laughter. Pancracio and Manteca vied with each other in calling forth oaths and obscenity.

XX

V ILLA is coming!"

The news spread like lightning. Villa—the magic word! The Great Man, the salient profile, the unconquerable warrior who, even at a distance, exerts the fascination of a reptile, a boa constrictor.

"Our Mexican Napoleon!" exclaimed Luis Cervantes.

"Yes! The Aztec Eagle! He buried his beak of steel in the head of Huerta the serpent!" Solís, Natera's chief of staff, remarked somewhat ironically, adding: "At least, that's how I expressed it in a speech I made at Ciudad Juárez!"

The two sat at the bar of the saloon, drinking beer. The "high hats," wearing mufflers around their necks and thick rough leather shoes on their feet, ate and drank endlessly. Their gnarled hands loomed across table, across bar. All their talk was of Villa and his men. The tales Natera's followers related won gasps of astonishment from Demetrio's men. Villa! Villa's battles! Ciudad Juárez . . . Tierra Blanca . . . Chihuahua . . . Torreón. . . .

The bare facts, the mere citing of observation and experience meant nothing. But the real story, with its extraordinary contrasts of high exploits and abysmal cruelties was quite different. Villa, indomitable lord of the sierra, the eternal victim of all governments . . . Villa tracked, hunted down like a wild beast . . . Villa the reincarnation of the old legend; Villa as Providence, the bandit, that passes through the world armed with the blazing torch of an ideal: to rob the rich and give to the poor. It was the poor who built up and imposed a legend about him which Time itself was to increase and embellish as a shining example from generation to generation.

"Look here, friend," one of Natera's men told Anastasio, "if General Villa takes a fancy to you, he'll give you

a ranch on the spot. But if he doesn't, he'll shoot
you down like a dog! God! You ought to see Villa's
troops! They're all northerners and dressed like lords!
You ought to see their wide-brimmed Texas hats and their
brand-new outfits and their four-dollar shoes, imported
from the U. S. A."

As they retailed the wonders of Villa and his men,
Natera's men gazed at one another ruefully, aware that
their own hats were rotten from sunlight and moisture,
that their own shirts and trousers were tattered and
barely fit to cover their grimy, lousy bodies.

"There's no such a thing as hunger up there. They
carry boxcars full of oxen, sheep, cows! They've got cars
full of clothing, trains full of guns, ammunition, food
enough to make a man burst!"

Then they spoke of Villa's airplanes.

"Christ, those planes! You know when they're close
to you, be damned if you know what the hell they are!
They look like small boats, you know, or tiny rafts . . .
and then pretty soon they begin to rise, making a hell of
a row. Something like an automobile going sixty miles an
hour. Then they're like great big birds that don't even
seem to move sometimes. But there's a joker! The Goddamn things have got some American fellow inside with
hand grenades by the thousand. Now you try and figure
what that means! The fight is on, see? You know how
a farmer feeds corn to his chickens, huh? Well, the American throws his lead bombs at the enemy just like that.
Pretty soon the whole damn field is nothing but a grave-
yard . . . dead men all over the dump . . . dead men here
. . . dead men there . . . dead men everywhere!"

Anastasio Montáñez questioned the speaker more par-
ticularly. It was not long before he realized that all this
high praise was hearsay and that not a single man in
Natera's army had ever laid eyes on Villa.

"Well, when you get down to it, I guess it doesn't mean
so much! No man's got much more guts than any other
man, if you ask me. All you need to be a good fighter is
pride, that's all. I'm not a professional soldier even though
I'm dressed like hell, but let me tell you. I'm not forced
to do this kind of bloody job, because I own . . ."

"Because I own over twenty oxen, whether you believe
it or not!" Quail said, mocking Anastasio.

XXI

THE firing lessened, then slowly died out. Luis Cervantes, who had been hiding amid a heap of ruins at the fortification on the crest of the hill, made bold to show his face. How he had managed to hang on, he did not know. Nor did he know when Demetrio and his men had disappeared. Suddenly he had found himself alone; then, hurled back by an avalanche of infantry, he fell from his saddle; a host of men trampled over him until he rose from the ground and a man on horseback hoisted him up behind him. After a few moments, horse and riders fell. Left without rifle, revolver, or arms of any kind, Cervantes found himself lost in the midst of white smoke and whistling bullets. A hole amid a debris of crumbling stone offered a refuge of safety.

"Hello, partner!"

"Luis, how are you!"

"The horse threw me. They fell upon me. Then they took my gun away. You see, they thought I was dead. There was nothing I could do!" Luis Cervantes explained apologetically. Then:

"Nobody threw me down," Solís said. "I'm here because I like to play safe."

The irony in Solís' voice brought a blush to Cervantes' cheek.

"By God, that chief of yours is a man!" Solís said. "What daring, what assurance! He left me gasping—and a hell of a lot of other men with more experience than me, too!"

Luis Cervantes vouchsafed no answer.

"What! Weren't you there? Oh, I see! You found a nice place for yourself at the right time. Come here, Luis, I'll explain; let's go behind that rock. From this meadow to the foot of the hill, there's no road save this path below. To the right, the incline is too sharp; you can't do

79

anything there. And it's worse to the left; the ascent is so
dangerous that a second's hesitation means a fall down
those rocks and a broken neck at the end of it. All right!
A number of men from Moya's brigade who went down to
the meadow decided to attack the enemy's trenches the
first chance they got. The bullets whizzed about us, the
battle raged on all sides. For a time they stopped firing,
so we thought they were being attacked from behind. We
stormed their trenches—look, partner, look at that
meadow! It's thick with corpses! Their machine guns did
that for us. They mowed us down like wheat; only a handful escaped. Those Goddamned officers went white as a
sheet; even though we had reinforcements they were
afraid to order a new charge. That was when Demetrio
Macías plunged in. Did he wait for orders? Not he! He
just shouted:

" 'Come on, boys! Let's go for them!'

" 'Damn fool!' I thought. 'What the hell does he think
he's doing!'

"The officers, surprised, said nothing. Demetrio's
horse seemed to wear eagle's claws instead of hoofs, it
soared so swiftly over the rocks. 'Come on! Come on!' his
men shouted, following him like wild deer, horses and
men welded into a mad stampede. Only one young fellow
stepped wild and fell headlong into the pit. In a few seconds the others appeared at the top of the hill, storming
the trenches and killing the Federals by the thousand.
With his rope, Demetrio lassoed the machine guns and
carried them off, like a bull herd throwing a steer. Yet his
success could not last much longer, for the Federals
were far stronger in numbers and could easily have destroyed Demetrio and his men. But we took advantage of
their confusion, we rushed upon them and they soon
cleared out of their position. That chief of yours is a
wonderful soldier!"

Standing on the crest of the hill, they could easily
sight one side of the Bufa peak. Its highest crag spread out
like the feathered head of a proud Aztec king. The three-
hundred-foot slope was literally covered with dead, their
hair matted, their clothes clotted with grime and blood.
A host of ragged women, vultures of prey, ranged over
the tepid bodies of the dead, stripping one man bare, de-

spoiling another, robbing from a third his dearest possessions.

Amid clouds of white rifle smoke and the dense black vapors of flaming buildings, houses with wide doors and windows bolted shone in the sunlight. The streets seemed to be piled upon one another, or wound picturesquely about fantastic corners, or set to scale the hills nearby. Above the graceful cluster of houses, rose the lithe columns of a warehouse and the towers and cupola of the church.

"How beautiful the revolution! Even in its most barbarous aspect it is beautiful," Solís said with deep feeling. Then a vague melancholy seized him, and speaking low:

"A pity what remains to do won't be as beautiful! We must wait a while, until there are no men left to fight on either side, until no sound of shot rings through the air save from the mob as carrion-like it falls upon the booty; we must wait until the psychology of our race, condensed into two words, shines clear and luminous as a drop of water: *Robbery! Murder!* What a colossal failure we would make of it, friend, if we, who offer our enthusiasm and lives to crush a wretched tyrant, became the builders of a monstrous edifice holding one hundred or two hundred thousand monsters of exactly the same sort. People without ideals! A tyrant folk! Vain bloodshed!"

Large groups of Federals pushed up the hill, fleeing from the "high hats." A bullet whistled past them, singing as it sped. After his speech, Alberto Solís stood lost in thought, his arms crossed. Suddenly, he took fright.

"I'll be damned if I like these plaguey mosquitoes!" he said. "Let's get away from here!"

So scornfully Luis Cervantes smiled that Solís sat down on a rock quite calm, bewildered. He smiled. His gaze roved as he watched the spirals of smoke from the rifles, the dust of roofs crumbling from houses as they fell before the artillery. He believed he discerned the symbol of the revolution in these clouds of dust and smoke that climbed upward together, met at the crest of the hill and, a moment after, were lost. . . .

"By heaven, now I see what it all means!"

He sketched a vast gesture, pointing to the station.

Locomotives belched huge clouds of black dense smoke rising in columns; the trains were overloaded with fugitives who had barely managed to escape from the captured town.

Suddenly he felt a sharp blow in the stomach. As though his legs were putty, he rolled off the rock. His ears buzzed. . . . Then darkness . . . silence . . . eternity. . . .

PART TWO

Demetrio, nonplussed, scratched his head: "Look here, don't ask me any more questions. . . . You gave me the eagle I wear on my hat, didn't you? All right then; you just tell me: 'Demetrio, do this or do that,' and that's all there is to it."

I

TO champagne, that sparkles and foams as the beaded bubbles burst at the brim of the glass, Demetrio preferred the native tequila, limpid and fiery.

The soldiers sat in groups about the tables in the restaurant, ragged men, filthy with sweat, dirt and smoke, their hair matted, wild, disheveled.

"I killed two colonels," one man clamored in a guttural harsh voice. He was a small fat fellow, with embroidered hat and chamois coat, wearing a light purple handkerchief about his neck.

"They were so Goddamned fat they couldn't even run. By God, I wish you could have seen them, tripping and stumbling at every step they took, climbing up the hill, red as tomatoes, their tongues hanging out like hounds. 'Don't run so fast, you lousy beggars!' I called after them. 'I'm not so fond of frightened geese—stop, you bald-headed bastards: I won't harm you! You needn't worry!' By God, they certainly fell for it. *Pop, pop!* One shot for each of them, and a well-earned rest for a pair of poor sinners, be damned to them!"

"I couldn't get a single one of their generals!" said a swarthy man who sat in one corner between the wall and the bar, holding his rifle between his outstretched legs. "I sighted one: a fellow with a hell of a lot of gold plastered all over him. His gold chevrons shone like a Goddamned sunset. And I let him go by, fool that I was. He took off his handkerchief and waved it. I stood there with my mouth wide open like a fool! Then I ducked and he started shooting, bullet after bullet. I let him kill a poor *cargador*. Then I said: 'My turn, now! Holy Virgin, Mother of God! Don't let me miss this son of a bitch.' But, by Christ, he disappeared. He was riding a hell of a fine nag; he went by me like lightning! There was another poor fool coming up the road. He got it and turned the prettiest somersault you ever saw!"

Talk flew from lip to lip, each soldier vying with his fellow, snatching the words from the other's mouth. As they declaimed passionately, women with olive, swarthy skins, bright eyes, and teeth of ivory, with revolvers at their waists, cartridge-belts across their breasts, and broad Mexican hats on their heads, wove their way like stray street curs in and out among groups. A vulgar wench, with rouged cheeks and dark brown arms and neck, gave a great leap and landed on the bar near Demetrio's table.

He turned his head toward her and literally collided with a pair of lubric eyes under a narrow forehead and thick, straight hair, parted in the middle.

The door opened wide. Anastasio, Pancracio, Quail, and Meco filed in, dazed.

Anastasio uttered a cry of surprise and stepped forward to shake hands with the little fat man wearing a *charro* suit and a lavender bandanna. A pair of old friends, met again. So warm was their embrace, so tightly they clutched each other that the blood rushed to their heads, they turned purple.

"Look here, Demetrio, I want the honor of introducing you to Blondie. He's a real friend, you know. I love him like a brother. You must get to know him, Chief, he's a man! Do you remember that damn jail at Escobedo, where we stayed together for over a year?"

Without removing his cigar from his lips, Demetrio, buried in a sullen silence amid the bustle and uproar, offered his hand and said:

"I'm delighted to meet you!"

"So your name is Demetrio Macías?" the girl asked suddenly. Seated on the bar, she swung her legs; at every swing, the toes of her shoes touched Demetrio's back.

"Yes: I'm Demetrio Macías!" he said, scarcely turning toward her.

Indifferently, she continued to swing her legs, displaying her blue stockings with ostentation.

"Hey, War Paint, what are you doing here? Step down and have a drink!" said the man called Blondie.

The girl accepted readily and boldly thrust her way through the crowd to a chair facing Demetrio.

"So you're the famous Demetrio Macías, the hero of Zacatecas?" the girl asked.

Demetrio bowed assent, while Blondie, laughing, said:

"You're a wise one, War Paint. You want to sport a general!"

Without understanding Blondie's words, Demetrio raised his eyes to hers; they gazed at each other like two dogs sniffing one another with distrust. Demetrio could not resist her furiously provocative glances; he was forced to lower his eyes.

From their seats, some of Natera's officers began to hurl obscenities at War Paint. Without paying the slightest attention, she said:

"General Natera is going to hand you out a little general's eagle. Put it here and shake on it, boy!"

She stuck out her hand at Demetrio and shook it with the strength of a man. Demetrio, melting to the congratulations raining down upon him, ordered champagne.

"I don't want no more to drink," Blondie said to the waiter, "I'm feeling sick. Just bring me some ice water."

"I want something to eat," said Pancracio. "Bring me anything you've got but don't make it chili or beans!"

Officers kept coming in; presently the restaurant was crowded. Small stars, bars, eagles and insignia of every sort or description dotted their hats. They wore wide silk bandannas around their necks, large diamond rings on their fingers, large heavy gold watch chains across their breasts.

"Here, waiter," Blondie cried, "I ordered ice water. And I'm not begging for it either, see? Look at this bunch of bills. I'll buy you, your wife, and all you possess, see? Don't tell me there's none left—I don't care a damn about that! It's up to you to find some way to get it and Goddamned quick, too. I don't like to play about; I get mad when I'm crossed. . . . By God, didn't I tell you I wouldn't stand for any backchat? You won't bring it to me, eh? Well, take this. . . ."

A heavy blow sent the waiter reeling to the floor.

"That's the sort of man I am, General Macías! I'm clean-shaven, eh? Not a hair on my chin? Do you know

why? Well, I'll tell you! You see I get mad easy as hell; and when there's nobody to pick on, I pull my hair until my temper passes. If I hadn't pulled my beard hair by hair, I'd have died a long time ago from sheer anger!"

"It does you no good to go to pieces when you're angry," a man affirmed earnestly from below a hat that covered his head as a roof does a house. "When I was up at Torreón I killed an old lady who refused to sell me some enchiladas. She was angry, I can tell you; I got no enchiladas but I felt satisfied anyhow!"

"I killed a storekeeper at Parral because he gave me some change and there were two Huerta bills in it," said a man with a star on his hat and precious stones on his black, calloused hands.

"Down in Chihuahua I killed a man because I always saw him sitting at the table whenever I went to eat. I hated the looks of him so I just killed him! What the hell could I do!"

"Hmm! I killed. . . ."

The theme is inexhaustible.

By dawn, when the restaurant was wild with joy and the floor dotted with spittle, young painted girls from the suburbs had mingled freely among the dark northern women. Demetrio pulled out his jeweled gold watch, asking Anastasio Montáñez to tell him the time.

Anastasio glanced at the watch, then, poking his head out of a small window, gazed at the starry sky.

"The Pleiades are pretty low in the west. I guess it won't be long now before daybreak. . . ."

Outside the restaurant, the shouts, laughter and song of the drunkards rang through the air. Men galloped wildly down the streets, the hoofs of their horses hammering on the sidewalks. From every quarter of the town pistols spoke, guns belched. Demetrio and the girl called War Paint staggered tipsily hand in hand down the center of the street, bound for the hotel.

II

"WHAT damned fools," said War Paint convulsed with laughter! "Where the hell do you come from? . . . Soldiers don't sleep in hotels and inns any more. . . . Where do you come from? You just go anywhere you like and pick a house that pleases you, see. When you go there, make yourself at home and don't ask anyone for anything. What the hell is the use of the revolution? Who's it for? For the folks who live in towns? We're the city folk now, see? Come on, Pancracio, hand me your bayonet. Damn these rich people, they lock up everything they've got!"

She dug the steel point through the crack of a drawer and, pressing on the hilt, broke the lock, opened the splinted cover of a writing desk. Anastasio, Pancracio and War Paint plunged their hands into a mass of post cards, photographs, pictures and papers, scattering them all over the rug. Finding nothing he wanted, Pancracio gave vent to his anger by kicking a framed photograph into the air with the toe of his shoe. It smashed on the candelabra in the center of the room.

They pulled their empty hands out of the heap of paper, cursing. But War Paint was of sterner stuff; tirelessly she continued to unlock drawer after drawer without failing to investigate a single spot. In their absorption, they did not notice a small gray velvet-covered box which rolled silently across the floor, coming to a stop at Luis Cervantes' feet.

Demetrio, lying on the rug, seemed to be asleep; Cervantes, who had watched everything with profound indifference, pulled the box closer to him with his foot, and stooping to scratch his ankle, swiftly picked it up. Something gleamed up at him, dazzling. It was two pure-water

89

diamonds mounted in filigreed platinum. Hastily he thrust them inside his coat pocket.

When Demetrio awoke, Cervantes said:

"General, look at the mess these boys have made here. Don't you think it would be advisable to forbid this sort of thing?"

"No. It's about their only pleasure after putting their bellies up as targets for the enemy's bullets."

"Yes, of course, General, but they could do it somewhere else. You see, this sort of thing hurts our prestige, and worse, our cause!"

Demetrio leveled his eagle eyes at Cervantes. He drummed with his fingernails against his teeth, absentmindedly. Then:

"Come along, now, don't blush," he said. "You can talk like that to someone else. We know what's mine is mine, what's yours is yours. You picked the box, all right; I picked my gold watch; all right too!"

His words dispelled any pretense. Both of them, in perfect harmony, displayed their booty.

War Paint and her companions were ransacking the rest of the house. Quail entered the room with a twelve-year-old girl upon whose forehead and arms were already marked copper-colored spots. They stopped short, speechless with surprise as they saw the books lying in piles on the floor, chairs and tables, the large mirrors thrown to the ground, smashed, the huge albums and the photographs torn into shreds, the furniture, *objets d'art* and bric-a-brac broken. Quail held his breath, his avid eyes scouring the room for booty.

Outside, in one corner of the patio, lost in dense clouds of suffocating smoke, Manteca was boiling corn on the cob, feeding his fire with books and paper that made the flames leap wildly through the air.

"Hey!" Quail shouted. "Look what I found. A fine sweat-cover for my mare."

With a swift pull he wrenched down a hanging, which fell over a handsomely carved upright chair.

"Look, look at all these naked women!" Quail's little companion cried, enchanted at a de luxe edition of Dante's *Divine Comedy*. "I like this; I think I'll take it along."

She began to tear out the illustrations which pleased her most.

Demetrio crossed the room and sat down beside Luis Cervantes. He ordered some beer, handed one bottle up to his secretary, downed his own bottle at one gulp. Then, drowsily, he half closed his eyes, and soon fell sound asleep.

"Hey!" a man called to Pancracio from the threshold. "When can I see your general?"

"You can't see him. He's got a hangover this morning. What the hell do you want?"

"I want to buy some of those books you're burning."

"I'll sell them to you myself."

"How much do you want for them?"

Pancracio frowned in bewilderment.

"Give me a nickel for those with pictures, see. I'll give you the rest for nothing if you buy all those with pictures."

The man returned with a large basket to carry away the books. . . .

"Come on, Demetrio, come on, you pig, get up! Look who's here! It's Blondie. You don't know what a fine man he is!"

"I like you very much, General Macías, and I like the way you do things. So if it's all right, I'd like very much to serve under you!"

"What's your rank?" Demetrio asked him.

"I'm a captain, General."

"All right, you can serve with me now. I'll make you major. How's that?"

Blondie was a round little fellow, with waxed mustache. When he laughed, his blue eyes disappeared mischievously between his forehead and his fat cheeks. He had been a waiter at "El Mónico," in Chihuahua; now he proudly wore three small brass bars, the insignia of his rank in the Northern Division.

Blondie showered eulogy after eulogy on Demetrio and his men; this proved sufficient reason for bringing out a fresh case of beer, which was finished in short order.

Suddenly War Paint reappeared in the middle of the room, wearing a beautiful silk dress covered with exquisite lace.

"You forgot the stockings," Blondie shouted, shaking with laughter. Quail's girl also burst out laughing. But War Paint did not care. She shrugged her shoulders indifferently, sat down on the floor, kicked off her white satin slippers, and wiggled her toes happily, giving their muscles a freedom welcome after their tight confinement in the slippers. She said:

"Hey, you, Pancracio, go and get me my blue stockings . . . they're with the rest of my plunder."

Soldiers and their friends, companions and veterans of other campaigns, began to enter in groups of twos and threes. Demetrio, growing excited, began to narrate in detail his most notable feats of arms.

"What the hell is that noise?" he asked in surprise as he heard string and brass instruments tuning up in the patio.

"General Demetrio Macías," Luis Cervantes said solemnly, "it's a banquet all of your old friends and followers are giving in your honor to celebrate your victory at Zacatecas and your well-merited promotion to the rank of general!"

III

"GENERAL MACÍAS, I want you to meet my future wife," Luis Cervantes said with great emphasis as he led a beautiful girl into the dining room.

They all turned to look at her. Her large blue eyes grew wide in wonder. She was barely fourteen. Her skin was like a rose, soft, pink, fresh; her hair was very fair; the expression in her eyes was partly impish curiosity, partly a vague childish fear. Perceiving that Demetrio eyed her like a beast of prey, Luis Cervantes congratulated himself.

They made room for her between Luis Cervantes and Blondie, opposite Demetrio.

Bottles of tequila, dishes of cut glass, bowls, porcelains and vases lay scattered over the table indiscriminately. Meco, carrying a box of beer upon his shoulders, came in cursing and sweating.

"You don't know this fellow Blondie yet," said War Paint, noticing the persistent glances he was casting at Luis Cervantes' bride. "He's a smart fellow, I can tell you, and he never misses a trick."

She gazed at him lecherously, adding:

"That's why I don't like to see him close, even on a photograph!"

The orchestra struck up a raucous march as though they were playing at a bullfight. The soldiers roared with joy.

"What fine tripe, General; I swear I haven't tasted the like of it in all my life," Blondie said, as he began to reminisce about "El Mónico" at Chihuahua.

"You really like it, Blondie?" responded Demetrio. "Go ahead, call for more, eat your bellyful."

"It's just the way I like it," Anastasio chimed in. "Yes, I like good food! But nothing really tastes good to you unless you belch!"

The noise of mouths being filled, of ravenous feeding followed. All drank copiously. At the end of the dinner, Luis Cervantes rose, holding a champagne glass in one hand, and said:

"General . . ."

"Ho!" War Paint interrupted. "This speech-making business isn't for me; I'm all against it. I'll go out to the corral since there's no more eating here."

Presenting Demetrio with a black velvet-covered box containing a small brass eagle, Luis Cervantes made a toast which no one understood but everyone applauded enthusiastically. Demetrio took the insignia in his hands; and with flushed face, and eyes shining, declared with great candor:

"What in hell am I going to do with this buzzard!"

"Compadre," Anastasio Montáñez said in a tremulous voice. "I ain't got much to tell you. . . ."

Whole minutes elapsed between his words; the cursed words would not come to Anastasio. His face, coated with filth, unwashed for days, turned crimson, shining with perspiration. Finally he decided to finish his toast at all costs. "Well, I ain't got much to tell you, except that we are pals. . . ."

Then, since everyone had applauded at the end of Luis Cervantes' speech, Anastasio, having finished, made a sign, and the company clapped their hands in great gravity.

But everything turned out for the best, since his awkwardness inspired others. Manteca and Quail stood up and made their toasts, too. When Meco's turn came, War Paint rushed in shouting jubilantly, attempting to drag a splendid black horse into the dining room.

"My booty! My booty!" she cried, patting the superb animal on the neck. It resisted every effort she made until a strong jerk of the rope and a sudden lash brought it in prancing smartly. The soldiers, half drunk, stared at the beast with ill-disguised envy.

"I don't know what the hell this she-devil's got, but she always beats everybody to it," cried Blondie. "She's been the same ever since she joined us at Tierra Blanca!"

"Hey, Pancracio, bring me some alfalfa for my horse,"

War Paint commanded crisply, throwing the horse's rope to one of the soldiers.

Once more they filled their glasses. Many a head hung low with fatigue or drunkenness. Most of the company, however, shouted with glee, including Luis Cervantes' girl. She had spilled all her wine on a handkerchief and looked all about her with blue wondering eyes.

"Boys," Blondie suddenly screamed, his shrill, guttural voice dominating the mall, "I'm tired of living; I feel like killing myself right now. I'm sick and tired of War Paint and this other little angel from heaven won't even look at me!"

Luis Cervantes saw that the last remark was addressed to his bride; with great surprise he realized that it was not Demetrio's foot he had noticed close to the girl's, but Blondie's. He was boiling with indignation.

"Keep your eye on me, boys," Blondie went on, gun in hand. "I'm going to shoot myself right in the forehead!"

He aimed at the large mirror on the opposite wall which gave back his whole body in reflection. He took careful aim. . . .

"Don't move, War Paint."

The bullet whizzed by, grazing War Paint's hair. The mirror broke into large jagged fragments. She did not even so much as blink.

IV

LATE in the afternoon Luis Cervantes rubbed his eyes and sat up. He had been sleeping on the hard pavement, close to the trunk of a fruit tree. Anastasio, Pancracio and Quail slept nearby, breathing heavily.

His lips were swollen, his nose dry and cold. There were bloodstains on his hands and shirt. At once he recalled what had taken place. Soon he rose to his feet and made for one of the bedrooms. He pushed at the door several times without being able to force it open. For a few minutes he stood there, hesitating.

No—he had not dreamed it. Everything had really occurred just as he recalled it. He had left the table with his bride and taken her to the bedroom, but just as he was closing the door, Demetrio staggered after them and made one leap toward them. Then War Paint dashed in after Demetrio and began to struggle with him. Demetrio, his eyes white-hot, his lips covered with long blond hairs, looked for the bride, in despair. But War Paint pushed him back vigorously.

"What the hell is the matter with you? What the hell are you trying to do?" he demanded, furious.

War Paint put her leg between his, twisted it suddenly, and Demetrio fell to the ground outside of the bedroom. He rose, raging.

"Help! Help! He's going to kill me!" she cried, seizing Demetrio's wrist and turning the gun aside. The bullet hit the floor. War Paint continued to shriek. Anastasio disarmed Demetrio from behind.

Demetrio, standing like a furious bull in the middle of the arena, cast fierce glances at all the bystanders, Luis Cervantes, Anastasio, Manteca, and the others.

"Goddamn you! You've taken my gun away! Christ! As if I needed any gun to beat the hell out of you."

96

Flinging out his arms, beating and pummeling, he felled everyone within reach. Down they rolled like tenpins. Then, after that, Luis Cervantes could remember nothing more. Perhaps his bride, terrified by all these brutes, had wisely vanished and hidden herself.

"Perhaps this bedroom communicates with the living room and I can go in through there," he thought, standing at the threshold. At the sound of his footsteps, War Paint woke up. She lay on the rug close to Demetrio at the foot of a couch filled with alfalfa and corn where the black horse had fed.

"What are you looking for? Oh, hell, I know what you want! Shame on *you!* Why, I had to lock up your sweetheart because I couldn't struggle any more against this damned Demetrio. Take the key, it's lying on that table, there!"

Luis Cervantes searched in vain all over the house.

"Come on, tell me all about your girl."

Nervously, Luis Cervantes continued to look for the key.

"Come on, don't be in such a hurry, I'll give it to you. Come along, tell me; I like to hear about these things, you know. That girl is your kind, she's not a country person like us."

"I've nothing to say. She's my girl and we're going to get married, that's all."

"Ho! Ho! Ho! You're going to marry her, eh? Trying to teach your grandmother to suck eggs, eh? Why, you fool, any place you just manage to get to for the first time in your life, I've left a hundred miles behind me, see. I've cut my wisdom teeth. It was Meco and Manteca who took the girl from her home: I knew that all the time. You just gave them something so as to have her yourself, gave them a pair of cuff links . . . or a miraculous picture of some Virgin. . . . Am I right? Sure, I am! There aren't so many people in the world who know what's what, but I reckon you'll meet up with a few before you die!"

War Paint got up to give him the key but she could not find it either. She was much surprised. Quickly, she ran to the bedroom door and peered through the keyhole, standing motionless until her eye grew accustomed to the darkness within. Without drawing away, she said:

"You damned Blondie. Son of a bitch! Come here a minute, look!"

She went away laughing.

"Didn't I tell them all I'd never seen a smarter fellow in all my life!"

The following morning, War Paint watched for the moment when Blondie left the bedroom to feed his horses. . . .

"Come on, Angel Face. Run home quick!"

The blue-eyed girl, with a face like a Madonna, stood naked save for her chemise and stockings. War Paint covered her with Manteca's lousy blanket, took her by the hand and led her to the street.

"God, I'm happy," War Paint cried. "I'm crazy . . . about Blondie . . . now."

V

LIKE neighing colts, playful when the rainy season begins, Demetrio's men galloped through the sierra.

"To Moyahua, boys. Let's go to Demetrio Macías' country!"

"To the country of Mónico the *cacique!*"

The landscape grew clearer; the sun margined the diaphanous sky with a fringe of crimson. Like the bony shoulders of immense sleeping monsters, the chains of mountains rose in the distance. Crags there were like heads of colossal native idols; others like giants' faces, their grimaces awe-inspiring or grotesque, calling forth a smile or a shudder at a presentment of mystery.

Demetrio Macías rode at the head of his men; behind him the members of his staff: Colonel Anastasio Montáñez, Lieutenant-Colonel Pancracio, Majors Luis Cervantes and Blondie. Still further behind came War Paint with Venancio, who paid her many compliments and recited the despairing verses of Antonio Plaza. As the sun's rays began to slip from the housetops, they made their entrance into Moyahua, four abreast, to the sound of the bugle. The roosters' chorus was deafening, dogs barked their alarm, but not a living soul stirred on the streets.

War Paint spurred her black horse and with one jump was abreast with Demetrio. They rode forward, elbow to elbow. She wore a silk dress and heavy gold earrings. Proudly her pale blue gown deepened her olive skin and the coppery spots on her face and arms. Riding astride, she had pulled her skirts up to her knees; her stockings showed, filthy and full of runs. She wore a gun at her side, a cartridge belt hung over the pommel of her saddle.

Demetrio was also dressed in his best clothes. His

broad-brimmed hat was richly embroidered; his leather trousers were tight-fitting and adorned with silver buttons; his coat was embroidered with gold thread.

There was a sound of doors being beaten down and forced open. The soldiers had already scattered through the town, to gather together ammunition and saddles from everywhere.

"We're going to bid Mónico good morning," Demetrio said gravely, dismounting and tossing his bridle to one of his men. "We're going to have breakfast with Don Mónico, who's a particular friend of mine. . . ."

The general's staff smiled . . . a sinister, malign smile. . . .

Making their spurs ring against the pavement, they walked toward a large pretentious house, obviously that of a *cacique*.

"It's closed airtight," Anastasio Montáñez said, pushing the door with all his might.

"That's all right. I'll open it," Pancracio answered, lowering his rifle and pointing it at the lock.

"No, no," Demetrio said, "knock first."

Three blows with the butt of the rifle. Three more. No answer. Pancracio disobeys orders. He fires, smashing the lock. The door opens. Behind, a confusion of skirts and children's bare legs rushing to and fro, pell-mell.

"I want wine. Hey, there: wine!" Demetrio cries in an imperious voice, pounding heavily on a table.

"Sit down, boys."

A lady peeps out, another, a third; from among black skirts, the heads of frightened children. One of the women, trembling, walks toward a cupboard and, taking out some glasses and a bottle, serves wine.

"What arms have you?" Demetrio demands harshly.

"Arms, arms . . . ?" the lady answers, a taste of ashes on her tongue. "What arms do you expect us to have! We are respectable, lonely old ladies!"

"Lonely, eh! Where's Señor Mónico?"

"Oh, he's not here, gentlemen, I assure you! We merely rent the house from him, you see. We only know him by name!"

Demetrio orders his men to search the house.

"No, please don't. We'll bring you whatever we have ourselves, but please for God's sake, don't do anything cruel. We're spinsters, lone women . . . perfectly respectable. . . ."

"Spinsters, hell! What about these kids here?" Pancracio interrupts brutally. "Did they spring from the earth?"

The women disappear hurriedly, to return with an old shotgun, covered with dust and cobwebs, and a pistol with rusty broken springs.

Demetrio smiles.

"All right, then, let's see the money. . . ."

"Money? Money? But what money do you think a couple of spinsters have? Spinsters alone in the world. . . . ?"

They glance up in supplication at the nearest soldier; but they are seized with horror. For they have just seen the Roman soldier who crucified Our Lord in the *Via Crucis* of the parish! They have seen Pancracio!

Demetrio repeats his order to search.

Once again the women disappear to return this time with a moth-eaten wallet containing a few Huerta bills.

Demetrio smiles and without further delay calls to his men to come in. Like hungry dogs who have sniffed their meat, the mob bursts in, trampling down the women who sought to bar the entrance with their bodies. Several faint, fall to the ground; others flee in panic. The children scream.

Pancracio is about to break the lock of a huge wardrobe when suddenly the doors open and out comes a man with a rifle in his hands.

"Señor Don Mónico!" they all exclaim in surprise.

"Demetrio, please, don't harm me! Please don't harm me! Please don't hurt me! You know, Señor Don Demetrio, I'm your friend!"

Demetrio Macías smiles slyly. "Are friends," he asked, "usually welcomed gun in hand?"

Don Mónico, in consternation, throws himself at Demetrio's feet, clasps his knees, kisses his shoes:

"My wife! . . . My children! . . . Please, Señor Don Demetrio, my friend!"

Demetrio with taut hand puts his gun back in the holster.

A painful silhouette crosses his mind. He sees a woman with a child in her arms walking over the rocks of the sierra in the moonlight. A house in flames. . . .

"Clear out. Everybody outside!" he orders darkly.

His staff obeys. Mónico and the ladies kiss his hands, weeping with gratitude. The mob in the street, talking and laughing, stands waiting for the general's permission to ransack the *cacique's* house.

"I know where they've buried their money but I won't tell," says a youngster with a basket in his hands.

"Hm! I know the right place, mind you," says an old woman carrying a burlap sack to hold whatever the good Lord will provide. "It's on top of something . . . there's a lot of trinkets nearby and then there's a small bag with mother-of-pearl around it. That's the thing to look for!"

"You ain't talking sense, woman," puts in a man. "They ain't such fools as to leave silver lying loose like that. I'm thinking they've got it buried in the well, in a leather bag."

The mob moves slowly; some carry ropes to tie about their bundles, others wooden trays. The women open out their aprons or shawls calculating their capacity. All give thanks to Divine Providence as they wait for their share of the booty.

When Demetrio announces that he will not allow looting and orders them to disband, the mob, disconsolate, obeys him, and soon scatters; but there is a dull rumor among the soldiers and no one moves from his place.

Annoyed, Demetrio repeats this order.

A young man, a recent recruit, his head turned by drink, laughs and walks boldly toward the door. But before he has reached the threshold, a shot lays him low. He falls like a bull pierced in the neck by the matador's sword. Motionless, his smoking gun in his hand, Demetrio waits for the soldiers to withdraw.

"Set fire to the house!" he orders Luis Cervantes when they reach their quarters.

With a curious eagerness Luis Cervantes does not transmit the order but undertakes the task in person.

Two hours later when the city square was black with smoke and enormous tongues of fire rose from Mónico's house, no one could account for the strange behavior of the general.

Two hours later, when the moon was high, Blondie and War Paint's soldiers arguing in a loud voice, came to ransack the cacique's corner and take all the articles they wanted.

VI

THEY established themselves in a large gloomy house, which likewise belonged to the *cacique* of Moyahua. The previous occupants had already left strong evidences in the patio, which had been converted into a manure pile. The walls, once whitewashed, were now faded and cracked, revealing the bare unbaked adobe; the floor had been torn up by the hoofs of animals; the orchard was littered with rotted branches and dead leaves. From the entrance one stumbled over broken bits of chairs and other furniture covered with dirt.

By ten o'clock, Luis Cervantes yawned with boredom, said good night to Blondie and War Paint, who were downing endless drinks on a bench in the square, and made for the barracks. The drawing room was alone furnished. As he entered, Demetrio, lying on the floor with his eyes wide open, trying to count the beams, gazed at him.

"It's you, eh? What's new? Come on, sit down."

Luis Cervantes first went over to trim the candle, then drew up a chair without a back, a coarse rag doing the duty of a wicker bottom. The legs of the chair squeaked. War Paint's black horse snorted and whirled its crupper in wide circles. Luis Cervantes sank into his seat.

"General, I wish to make my report. Here you have . . ."

"Look here, man, I didn't really want this done, you know. Moyahua is almost like my native town. They'll say this is why we've been fighting!" Demetrio said, looking at the bulging sack of silver Cervantes was passing to him. Cervantes left his seat to squat down by Demetrio's side.

He stretched a blanket over the floor and into it poured the ten-peso pieces, shining, burning gold.

"First of all, General, only you and I know about this. . . . Secondly, you know well enough that if the sun shines, you should open the window. It's shining in our faces now but what about tomorrow? You should always look ahead. A bullet, a bolting horse, even a wretched cold in the head, and then there are a widow and orphans left in absolute want! . . . The Government? Ha! Ha! . . . Just go see Carranza or Villa or any of the big chiefs and try and tell them about your family. . . . If they answer with a kick you know where, they'll say they're giving you a handful of jewels. And they're right; we did not rise up in arms to make some Carranza or Villa President of our Republic. No—we fought to defend the sacred rights of the people against the tyranny of some vile *cacique*. And so, just as Villa or Carranza aren't going to ask our consent to the payment they're getting for the services they're rendering the country, we for our part don't have to ask anybody's permission about anything either."

Demetrio half stood up, grasped a bottle that stood nearby, drained it, then spat out the liquor, swelling out his cheeks.

"By God, my boy, you've certainly got the gift of gab!"

Luis felt dizzy, faint. The spattered beer seemed to intensify the stench of the refuse on which they sat; a carpet of orange and banana peels, fleshlike slices of watermelon, moldy masses of mangoes and sugarcane, all mixed up with cornhusks from tamales and human offal.

Demetrio's calloused hands shuffled through the brilliant coins, counting and counting. Recovering from his nausea, Luis Cervantes pulled out a small box of Fallières phosphate and poured forth rings, brooches, pendants, and countless valuable jewels.

"Look here, General, if this mess doesn't blow over (and it doesn't look as though it would), if the revolution keeps on, there's enough here already for us to live on abroad quite comfortably."

Demetrio shook his head.

"You wouldn't do that!"

"Why not? What are we staying on for? . . . What cause are we defending now?"

"That's something I càn't explain, Tenderfoot. But I'm thinking it wouldn't show much guts."

"Take your choice, General," said Luis Cervantes, pointing to the jewels which he had set in a row.

"Oh, you keep it all. . . . Certainly! . . . You know, I don't really care for money at all. I'll tell you the truth! I'm the happiest man in the world, so long as there's always something to drink and a nice little wench that catches my eye. . . ."

"Ha! Ha! You make the funniest jokes, General. Why do you stand for that snake of a War Paint, then?"

"I'll tell you, Tenderfoot, I'm fed up with her. But I'm like that: I just can't tell her so. I'm not brave enough to tell her to go plumb to hell. That's the way I am, see? When I like a woman, I get plain silly; and if she doesn't start something, I've not got the courage to do anything myself." He sighed. "There's Camilla at the ranch for instance. . . . Now, she's not much on looks, I know, but there's a woman I'd like to have. . . ."

"Well, General, we'll go and get her any day you like."

Demetrio winked maliciously.

"I promise you I'll do it."

"Are you sure? Do you really mean it? Look here, if you pull that off for me, I'll give you the watch and chain you're hankering after."

Luis Cervantes' eyes shone. He took the phosphate box, heavy with its contents, and stood up smiling.

"I'll see you tomorrow," he said. "Good night, General! Sleep well."

VII

I DON'T know any more about it than you do. The General told me, 'Quail, saddle your horse and my black mare and follow Cervantes; he's going on an errand for me.' Well, that's what happened. We left here at noon, and reached the ranch early that evening. One-eyed María Antonia took us in. . . . She asked after you, Pancracio. Next morning Luis Cervantes wakes me up. 'Quail, Quail, saddle the horses. Leave me mine but take the General's mare back to Moyahua. I'll catch up after a bit.' The sun was high when he arrived with Camilla. She got off and we stuck her on the General's mare."

"Well, and her? What sort of a face did she make coming back?" one of the men inquired.

"Hum! She was so damned happy she was gabbing all the way."

"And the tenderfoot?"

"Just as quiet as he always is, you know him."

"I think," Venancio expressed his opinion with great seriousness, "that if Camilla woke up in the General's bed, it was just a mistake. We drank a lot, remember! That alcohol went to our heads; we must have lost our senses."

"What the hell do you mean: alcohol! It was all cooked up between Cervantes and the General."

"Certainly! That city dude's nothing but a . . ."

"I don't like to talk about friends behind their backs," said Blondie, "but I can tell you this: one of the two sweethearts he had, one was mine, and the other was for the General."

They burst into guffaws of laughter.

When War Paint realized what had happened, she sought out Camilla and spoke with great affection:

"Poor little child! Tell me how all this happened."

Camilla's eyes were red from weeping.

"He lied to me! He lied! He came to the ranch and he told me, 'Camilla, I came just to get you. Do you want to go away with me?' You can be sure I wanted to go with him; when it comes to loving, I adore him. Yes, I adore him. Look how thin I've grown just pining away for him. Mornings I used to loathe to grind corn, Mamma ·would call me to eat, and anything I put in my mouth had no taste at all."

Once more she burst into tears, stuffing the corner of her apron into her mouth to drown her sobs.

"Look here, I'll help you out of this mess. Don't be silly, child, don't cry. Don't think about the dude any more! Honest to God, he's not worth it. You surely know his game, dear? . . . That's the only reason why the General stands for him. What a goose! . . . All right, you want to go back home?"

"The Holy Virgin protect me. My mother would beat me to death!"

"She'll do nothing of the sort. You and I can fix things. Listen! The soldiers are leaving any moment now. When Demetrio tells you to get ready, you tell him you feel pains all over your body as though someone had hit you; then you lie down and start yawning and shivering. Then put your hand on your forehead and say, 'I'm burning up with fever.' I'll tell Demetrio to leave us both here, that I'll stay to take care of you, that as soon as you're feeling all right again, we'll catch up with them. But instead of that, I'll see that you get home safe and sound."

VIII

THE sun had set, the town was lost in the drab melancholy of its ancient streets amid the frightened silence of its inhabitants, who had retired very early, when Luis Cervantes reached Primitivo's general store, his arrival interrupting a party that promised great doings.

Demetrio was engaged in getting drunk with his old comrades. The entire space before the bar was occupied. War Paint and Blondie had tied up their horses outside; but the other officers had stormed in brutally, horses and all. Embroidered hats with enormous and concave brims bobbed up and down everywhere. The horses wheeled about, prancing; tossing their restive heads; their fine breed showing in their black eyes, their small ears and dilating nostrils. Over the infernal din of the drunkards, the heavy breathing of the horses, the stamp of their hoofs on the tiled floor, and occasionally a quick, nervous whinny rang out.

A trivial episode was being commented upon when Luis Cervantes came in. A man, dressed in civilian clothes, with a round, black, bloody hole in his forehead, lay stretched out in the middle of the street, his mouth gaping. Opinion was at first divided but finally all concurred with Blondie's sound reasoning. The poor dead devil lying out there was the church sexton. . . . But what an idiot! His own fault, of course! Who in the name of hell could be so foolish as to dress like a city dude, with trousers, coat, cap, and all? Pancracio simply could not bear the sight of a city man in front of him! And that was that!

Eight musicians, playing wind instruments, interrupted their labors at Cervantes' command. Their faces were round and red as suns; their eyes popping, for they had been blowing on their brass instruments since dawn.

"General," Luis said pushing his way through the men on horseback, "a messenger has arrived with orders to proceed immediately to the pursuit and capture of Orozco and his men."

Faces that had been dark and gloomy were now illumined with joy.

"To Jalisco, boys!" cried Blondie, pounding on the counter.

"Make ready, all you darling Jalisco girls of my heart, for I'm coming along too!" Quail shouted, twisting back the brim of his hat.

The enthusiasm and rejoicing were general. Demetrio's friends, in the excitement of drunkenness, offered their services. Demetrio was so happy that he could scarcely speak. They were going to fight Orozco and his men! At last, they would pit themselves against real men! At last they would stop shooting down the Federals like so many rabbits or wild turkeys.

"If I could get hold of Orozco alive," Blondie said, "I'd rip off the soles of his feet and make him walk twenty-four hours over the sierra!"

"Was that the guy who killed Madero?" asked Meco.

"No," Blondie replied solemnly, "but once when I was a waiter at 'El Mónico,' up in Chihuahua, he hit me in the face!"

"Give Camilla the roan mare," Demetrio ordered Pancracio, who was already saddling the horses.

"Camilla can't go!" said War Paint promptly.

"Who in hell asked for your opinion?" Demetrio retorted angrily.

"It's true, isn't it, Camilla? You were sore all over, weren't you? And you've got a fever right now?"

"Well—anything Demetrio says."

"Don't be a fool! say *'No,'* come on, say *'No,'*" War Paint whispered nervously into Camilla's ear.

"I'll tell you, War Paint. . . . It's funny, but I'm beginning to fall for him. . . . Would you believe it!" Camilla whispered back.

War Paint turned purple, her cheeks swelled. Without a word she went out to get her horse that Blondie was saddling.

IX

A WHIRLWIND of dust, scorching down the road, suddenly broke into violent diffuse masses; and Demetrio's army emerged, a chaos of horses, broad chests, tangled manes, dilated nostrils, oval, wide eyes, hoofs flying in the air, legs stiffened from endless galloping; and of men with bronze faces, ivory teeth, and flashing eyes, their rifles in their hands or slung across the saddles.

Demetrio and Camilla brought up the rear. She was still nervous, white-lipped and parched; he was angry at their futile maneuver. For there had been battles, no followers of Orozco's to be seen. A handful of Federals, routed. A poor devil of a priest left dangling from a mesquite; a few dead, scattered over the field, who had once been united under the archaic slogan, *RIGHTS AND RELIGION*, with, on their breasts, the red cloth insignia: *Halt! The Sacred Heart of Jesus is with me!*

"One good thing about it is that I've collected all my back pay," Quail said, exhibiting some gold watches and rings stolen from the priest's house.

"It's fun fighting this way," Manteca cried, spicing every other word with an oath. "You know why the hell you're risking your hide."

In the same hand with which he held the reins, he clutched a shining ornament that he had torn from one of the holy statues.

After Quail, an expert in such matters, had examined Manteca's treasure covetously, he uttered a solemn guffaw.

"Hell, your ornament is nothing but tin!"

"Why in hell are you hanging on to that poison?" Pancracio asked Blondie who appeared dragging a prisoner.

"Do you want to know why? Because it's a long time

111

since I've had a good look at a man's face when a rope tightens around his neck!"

The fat prisoner breathed with difficulty as he followed Blondie on foot; his face was sunburnt, his eyes red; his forehead beaded with sweat, his wrists tightly bound together.

"Here, Anastasio, lend me your lasso. Mine's not strong enough; this bird will bust it. No, by God, I've changed my mind, friend Federal: think I'll kill you on the spot, because you are pulling too hard. Look, all the mesquites are still a long way off and there are no telegraph poles to hang you to!"

Blondie pulled his gun out, pressed the muzzle against the prisoner's chest and brought his finger against the trigger slowly . . . slowly. . . . The prisoner turned pale as a corpse; his face lengthened; his eyelids were fixed in a glassy stare. He breathed in agony, his whole body shook as with ague. Blondie kept his gun in the same position for a moment long as all eternity. His eyes shone queerly. An expression of supreme pleasure lit up his fat puffy face.

"No, friend Federal," he drawled, putting back his gun into the holster; "I'm not going to kill you just yet. . . . I'll make you my orderly. You'll see that I'm not so hardhearted!"

Slyly he winked at his companions. The prisoner had turned into an animal; he gulped, panting, dry-mouthed. Camilla, who had witnessed the scene, spurred her horse and caught up with Demetrio.

"What a brute that Blondie is: you ought to see what he did to a wretched prisoner," she said. Then she told Demetrio what had occurred. The latter wrinkled his brow but made no answer.

War Paint called Camilla aside.

"Hey you . . . what are you gabbling about? Blondie's my man, understand? From now on, you know how things are: whatever you've got against him you've got against me too! I'm warning you."

Camilla, frightened, hurried back to Demetrio's side.

X

THE men camped in a meadow, near three small
lone houses standing in a row, their white walls cutting
the purple fringe of the horizon. Demetrio and Camilla
rode toward them. Inside the corral a man, clad in shirt
and trousers of cheap white cloth, sat greedily puffing at
a cornhusk cigarette. Another man sitting beside him
on a flat cut stone was shelling corn. Kicking the air
with one dry, withered leg, the extremity of which was
like a goat's hoof, he frightened the chickens away.

"Hurry up, 'Pifanio," said the man who was smoking,
"the sun has gone down already and you haven't taken
the animals to water."

A horse neighed outside the corral; both men glanced
up in amazement. Demetrio and Camilla were looking
over the corral wall at them.

"I just want a place to sleep for my woman and me,"
Demetrio said reassuringly.

As he explained that he was the chief of a small
army which was to camp nearby that night, the man
smoking, who owned the place, bid them enter with great
deference. He ran to fetch a broom and a pail of water
to dust and wash the best corner of the hut as decent
lodging for his distinguished guests.

"Here, 'Pifanio, go out there and unsaddle the horses."

The man who was shelling corn stood up with an
effort. He was clad in a tattered shirt and vest. His
torn trousers, split at the seam, looked like the wings of
a cold, stricken bird; two strings of cloth dangled from
his waist. As he walked, he described grotesque circles.

"Surely you're not fit to do any work!" Demetrio said,
refusing to allow him to touch the saddles.

"Poor man," the owner cried from within the hut,
"he's lost all his strength. . . . But he surely works for
his pay. . . . He starts working the minute God Almighty

113

himself gets up, and it's after sundown now but he's
working still!"

Demetrio went out with Camilla for a stroll about
the encampment. The meadow, golden, furrowed, stripped
even of the smallest bushes, extended limitless in its immense desolation. The three tall ash trees which stood
in front of the small house, with dark green crests, round
and waving, with rich foliage and branches drooping to
the very ground, seemed a veritable miracle.

"I don't know why but I feel there's a lot of sadness
around here," said Demetrio.

"Yes," Camilla answered, "I feel that way too."

On the bank of a small stream, 'Pifanio was strenu-
ously tugging at a rope with a large can tied to the end
of it. He poured a stream of water over a heap of fresh,
cool grass; in the twilight, the water glimmered like crystal. A thin cow, a scrawny nag, and a burro drank noisily
together.

Demetrio recognized the limping servant and asked
him: "How much do you get a day?"

"Eight cents a day, boss."

He was an insignificant, scrofulous wraith of a man
with green eyes and straight, fair hair. He whined com-
plaint of his boss, the ranch, his bad luck, his dog's life.

"You certainly earn your pay all right, my lad," Demetrio interrupted kindly. "You complain and complain,
but you aren't no loafer, you work and work." Then,
aside to Camilla: "There's always more damned fools in
the valley than among us folk in the sierra, don't you
think?"

"Of course!" she replied.

They went on. The valley was lost in darkness; stars
came out. Demetrio put his arm around Camilla's waist
amorously and whispered in her ear.

"Yes," she answered in a faint voice.

She was indeed beginning to "fall for him" as she had
expressed it.

Demetrio slept badly. He flung out of the house very
early.

"Something is going to happen to me," he thought.

It was a silent dawn, with faint murmurs of joy. A
thrush sang timidly in one of the ash trees. The animals

in the corral trampled on the refuse. The pig grunted its somnolence. The orange tints of the sun streaked the sky; the last star flickered out.

Demetrio walked slowly to the encampment.

He was thinking of his plow, his two black oxen— young beasts they were, who had worked in the fields only two years—of his two acres of well-fertilized corn. The face of his young wife came to his mind, clear and true as life: he saw her strong, soft features, so gracious when she smiled on her husband, so proudly fierce toward strangers. But when he tried to conjure up the image of his son, his efforts were vain; he had forgotten. . . .

He reached the camp. Lying among the furrows, the soldiers slept with the horses, heads bowed, eyes closed.

"Our horses are pretty tired, Anastasio. I think we ought to stay here at least another day."

"Well, Compadre Demetrio, I'm hankering for the sierra. . . . If you only knew. . . . You may not believe me but nothing strikes me right here. I don't know what I miss but I know I miss something. I feel sad . . . lost. . . ."

"How many hours' ride from here to Limón?"

"It's no matter of hours; it's three days' hard riding, Demetrio."

"You know," Demetrio said softly, "I feel as though I'd like to see my wife again!"

Shortly after, War Paint sought out Camilla.

"That's one on you, my dear. . . . Demetrio's going to leave you flat! He told me so himself; 'I'm going to get my real woman,' he says, and he says, 'Her skin is white and tender . . . and her rosy cheeks. . . . How beautiful she is!' But you don't have to leave him, you know; if you're set on staying, well—they've got a child, you know, and I suppose you could drag it around. . . ."

When Demetrio returned, Camilla, weeping, told him everything.

"Don't pay no attention to that crazy baggage. It's all lies, lies!"

Since Demetrio did not go to Limón or remember his wife again, Camilla grew very happy. War Paint had merely stung herself, like a scorpion. . . .

XI

BEFORE dawn, they left for Tepatitlán. Their silhouettes wavered indistinctly over the road and the fields that bordered it, rising and falling with the monotonous, rhythmical gait of their horses, then faded away in the nacreous light of the swooning moon that bathed the valley.

Dogs barked in the distance.

"By noon we'll reach Tepatitlán, Cuquío tomorrow, and then . . . on to the sierra!" Demetrio said.

"Don't you think it advisable to go to Aguascalientes first, General?" Luis Cervantes asked.

"What for?"

"Our funds are melting slowly."

"Nonsense . . . forty thousand pesos in eight days!"

"Well, you see, just this week we recruited over five hundred new men; all the money's gone in advance loans and gratuities," Luis Cervantes answered in a low voice.

"No! We'll go straight to the sierra. We'll see later on."

"Yes, to the sierra!" many of the men shouted.

"To the sierra! To the sierra! Hurrah for the mountains!"

The plains seemed to torture them; they spoke with enthusiasm, almost with delirium, of the sierra. They thought of the mountains as of a most desirable mistress long since unvisited.

Dawn broke behind a cloud of fine reddish dust; the sun rose an immense curtain of fiery purple. Luis Cervantes pulled his reins and waited for Quail.

"What's the last word on our deal, Quail?"

"I told you, Tenderfoot: two hundred for the watch alone."

117

"No! I'll buy the lot: watches, rings, everything else. How much?"

Quail hesitated, turned slightly pale; then he cried spiritedly:

"Two thousand in bills, for the whole business!"

Luis Cervantes gave himself away. His eyes shone with such an obvious greed that Quail recanted and said:

"Oh, I was just fooling you. I won't sell nothing! Just the watch, see? And that's only because I owe Pancracio two hundred. He beat me at cards last night!"

Luis Cervantes pulled out four crisp "double-face" bills of Villa's issue and placed them in Quail's hands.

"I'd like to buy the lot. . . . Besides, nobody will offer you more than that!"

As the sun began to beat down upon them, Manteca suddenly shouted:

"Ho, Blondie, your orderly says he doesn't care to go on living. He says he's too damned tired to walk."

The prisoner had fallen in the middle of the road, utterly exhausted.

"Well, well!" Blondie shouted, retracing his steps. "So little mama's boy is tired, eh? Poor little fellow. I'll buy a glass case and keep you in a corner of my house just as if you were the Virgin Mary's own little son. You've got to reach home first, see? So I'll help you a little, sonny!"

He drew his sword out and struck the prisoner several times.

"Let's have a look at your rope, Pancracio," he said. There was a strange gleam in his eyes. Quail observed that the prisoner no longer moved arm or leg. Blondie burst into a loud guffaw: "The Goddamned fool. Just as I was learning him to do without food, too!"

"Well, mate, we're almost to Guadalajara," Venancio said, glancing over the smiling row of houses in Tepatitlán nestling against the hillside.

They entered joyously. From every window rosy cheeks, dark luminous eyes observed them. The schools were quickly converted into barracks; Demetrio found lodging in the chapel of an abandoned church.

The soldiers scattered about as usual pretending to seek arms and horses, but in reality for the sole purpose of looting.

In the afternoon some of Demetrio's men lay stretched out on the church steps, scratching their bellies. Venancio, his chest and shoulders bare, was gravely occupied in killing the fleas in his shirt. A man drew near the wall and sought permission to speak to the commander. The soldiers raised their heads; but no one answered.

"I'm a widower, gentlemen. I've got nine children and I barely make a living with the sweat of my brow. Don't be hard on a poor widower!"

"Don't you worry about women, Uncle," said Meco, who was rubbing his feet with tallow, "we've got War Paint here with us; you can have her for nothin'."

The man smiled bitterly.

"She's only got one fault," Pancracio observed, stretched out on the ground, staring at the blue sky, "she goes mad over any man she sees."

They laughed loudly; but Venancio with utmost gravity pointed to the chapel door. The stranger entered timidly and confided his troubles to Demetrio. The soldiers had cleaned him out; they had not left a single grain of corn.

"Why did you let them?" Demetrio asked indolently.

The man persisted, lamenting and weeping. Luis Cervantes was about to throw him out with an insult. But Camilla intervened.

"Come on, Demetrio, don't be harsh, give him an order to get his corn back."

Luis Cervantes was obliged to obey; he scrawled a few lines to which Demetrio appended an illegible scratch.

"May God repay you, my child! God will lead you to heaven that you may enjoy his glory. Ten bushels of corn are barely enough for this year's food!" the man cried, weeping for gratitude. Then he took the paper, kissed everybody's hand, and withdrew.

XII

THEY had almost reached Cuquío, when Anastasio Montáñez rode up to Demetrio: "Listen, Compadre, I almost forgot to tell you. . . . You ought to have seen the wonderful joke that man Blondie played. You know what he did with the old man who came to complain about the corn we'd taken away for horses? Well, the old man took the paper and went to the barracks. 'Right you are, brother, come in,' said Blondie, 'come in, come in here; to give you back what's yours is only the right thing to do. How many bushels did we steal? Ten? Sure it wasn't more than ten? . . . That's right, about fifteen, eh? Or was it twenty, perhaps? . . . Try and remember, friend. . . . Of course you're a poor man, aren't you, and you've a lot of kids to raise. . . . Yes, twenty it was. All right, now! It's not ten or fifteen or twenty I'm going to give you. You're going to count for yourself. . . . One, two, three . . . and when you've had enough you just·tell me and I'll stop.' And Blondie pulled out his sword and beat him till he cried for mercy."

War Paint rocked in her saddle, convulsed with mirth. Camilla, unable to control herself, blurted out:

"The beast! His heart's rotten to the core! No wonder I loathe him!"

At once War Paint's expression changed.

"What the hell is it to you!" she scowled. Camilla, frightened, spurred her horse forward. War Paint did likewise and, as she trotted past Camilla, suddenly she reached out, seized the other's hair and pulled with all her might. Camilla's horse shied; Camilla, trying to brush her hair back from over her eyes, abandoned the reins. She hesitated, lost her balance and fell in the road, striking her forehead against the stones.

War Paint, weeping with laughter, pressed on with utmost skill and caught Camilla's horse.

"Come on, Tenderfoot; here's a job for you," Pancracio said as he saw Camilla on Demetrio's saddle, her face covered with blood.

Luis Cervantes hurried toward her with some cotton; but Camilla, choking down her sobs and wiping her eyes, said hoarsely:

"Not from you! If I was dying, I wouldn't accept anything from you . . . not even water."

In Cuquío Demetrio received a message.

"We've got to go back to Tepatitlán, General," said Luis Cervantes, scanning the dispatch rapidly. "You've got to leave the men there while you go to Lagos and take the train over to Aguascalientes."

There was much heated protest, the men muttering to themselves or even groaning out loud. Some of them, mountaineers, swore that they would not continue with the troop.

Camilla wept all night. On the morrow at dawn, she begged Demetrio to let her return home.

"If you don't like me, all right," he answered sullenly.

"That's not the reason. I care for you a lot, really. But you know how it is. That woman . . ."

"Never mind about her. It's all right! I'll send her off to hell today. I had already decided that."

Camilla dried her tears. . . .

Every horse was saddled; the men were waiting only for orders from the Chief. Demetrio went up to War Paint and said under his breath:

"You're not coming with us."

"What!" she gasped.

"You're going to stay here or go wherever you damn well please, but you're not coming along with us."

"What? What's that you're saying?" Still she could not catch Demetrio's meaning. Then the truth dawned upon her. "You want to send me away? By God, I suppose you believe all the filth that bitch . . ."

And War Paint proceeded to insult Camilla, Luis Cervantes, Demetrio, and anyone she happened to remember at the moment, with such power and originality that the soldiers listened in wonder to vituperation that transcended their wildest dream of profanity and filth.

Demetrio waited a long time patiently. Then, as she showed no sign of stopping, he said to a soldier quite calmly:

"Throw this drunken woman out."

"Blondie, Blondie, love of my life! Help! Come and show them you're a real man! Show them they're nothing but sons of bitches! . . ."

She gesticulated, kicked, and shouted.

Blondie appeared; he had just got up. His blue eyes blinked under heavy lids; his voice rang hoarse. He asked what had occurred; someone explained. Then he went up to War Paint, and with great seriousness, said:

"Yes? Really? Well, if you want my opinion, I think this is just what ought to happen. So far as I'm concerned, you can go straight to hell. We're all fed up with you, see?"

War Paint's face turned to granite; she tried to speak but her muscles were rigid.

The soldiers laughed. Camilla, terrified, held her breath.

War Paint stared slowly at everyone about her. It all took no more than a few seconds. In a trice she bent down, drew a sharp, gleaming dagger from her stocking and leapt at Camilla.

A shrill cry. A body fell, the blood spurting from it.

"Kill her, Goddamn it," cried Demetrio, beyond himself. "Kill her!"

Two soldiers fell upon War Paint, but she brandished her dagger, defying them to touch her:

"Not the likes of you, Goddamn you! Kill me yourself, Demetrio!"

War Paint stepped forward, surrendered her dagger and, thrusting her breast forward, let her arms fall to her side.

Demetrio picked up the dagger, red with blood, but his eyes clouded; he hesitated, took a step backward. Then, with a heavy hoarse voice he growled, enraged:

"Get out of here! Quick!"

No one dared stop her. She moved off slowly, mute, somber.

Blondie's shrill, guttural voice broke the silent stupor:

"Thank God! At last I'm rid of that damned louse!"

XIII

Someone plunged a knife
Deep in my side.
Did he know why?
I don't know why.
Maybe he knew,
I never knew.
The blood flowed out
Of that mortal wound.
Did he know why?
I don't know why.
Maybe he knew,
I never knew.

His head lowered, his hands crossed over the pommel of his saddle, Demetrio in melancholy accents sang the strains of the intriguing song. Then he fell silent; for quite a while he continued to feel oppressed and sad.

"You'll see, as soon as we reach Lagos you'll come out of it, General. There's plenty of pretty girls to give us a good time," Blondie said.

"Right now I feel like getting damn drunk," Demetrio answered, spurring his horse forward and leaving them as if he wished to abandon himself entirely to his sadness.

After many hours of riding he called Cervantes.

"Listen, Tenderfoot, why in hell do we have to go to Aguascalientes?"

"You have to vote for the Provisional President of the Republic, General!"

"President, what? Who in the devil, then, is this man Carranza? I'll be damned if I know what it's all about."

At last they reached Lagos. Blondie bet that he would make Demetrio laugh that evening.

Trailing his spurs noisily over the pavement, Demetrio entered "El Cosmopolita" with Luis Cervantes, Blondie, and his assistants.

The civilians, surprised in their attempt to escape, remained where they were. Some feigned to return to their tables to continue drinking and talking; others hesitantly stepped up to present their respects to the commander.

"General, so pleased! . . . Major! Delighted to meet you!"

"That's right! I love refined and educated friends," Blondie said. "Come on, boys," he added, jovially drawing his gun, "I'm going to play a tune that'll make you all dance."

A bullet ricocheted on the cement floor passing between the legs of the tables, and the smartly dressed young men-about-town began to jump much as a woman jumps when frightened by a mouse under her skirt. Pale as ghosts, they conjured up wan smiles of obsequious approval. Demetrio barely parted his lips, but his followers doubled over with laughter.

"Look, Blondie," Quail shouted, "look at that man going out there. Look, he's limping."

"I guess the bee stung him all right."

Blondie, without turning to look at the wounded man, announced with enthusiasm that he could shoot off the top of a tequila bottle at thirty paces without aiming.

"Come on, friend, stand up," he said to the waiter. He dragged him out by the hand to the patio of the hotel and set a tequila bottle on his head. The poor devil refused. Insane with fright, he sought to escape, but Blondie pulled his gun and took aim.

"Come on, you son of a sea cook! If you keep on I'll give you a nice warm one!"

Blondie went to the opposite wall, raised his gun and fired. The bottle broke into bits, the alcohol poured over the lad's ghastly face.

"Now it's a go," cried Blondie, running to the bar to get another bottle, which he placed on the lad's head.

He returned to his former position, he whirled about, and shot without aiming. But he hit the waiter's ear instead of the bottle. Holding his sides with laughter, he said to the young waiter:

"Here, kid, take these bills. It ain't much. But you'll be all right with some alcohol and arnica."

After drinking a great deal of alcohol and beer, Demetrio spoke:

"Pay the bill, Blondie, I'm going to leave you."

"I ain't got a penny, General, but that's all right. I'll fix it. How much do we owe you, friend?"

"One hundred and eighty pesos, Chief," the bartender answered amiably.

Quickly, Blondie jumped behind the bar and with a sweep of both arms, knocked down all the glasses and bottles.

"Send the bill to General Villa, understand?"

He left, laughing loudly at his prank.

"Say there, you, where do the girls hang out?" Blondie asked, reeling up drunkenly toward a small well-dressed man, standing at the door of a tailor shop.

The man stepped down to the sidewalk politely to let Blondie pass.

Blondie stopped and looked at him curiously, impertinently.

"Little boy, you're very small and dainty, ain't you? . . . No? . . . Then I'm a liar! . . . That's right! . . . You know the puppet dance. . . . You don't? The hell you don't! . . . I met you in a circus! I know you can even dance on a tightrope! . . . You watch!"

Blondie drew his gun out and began to shoot, aiming at the tailor's feet; the tailor gave a little jump at every pull of the trigger.

"See! You do know how to dance on the tightrope, don't you?"

Taking his friends by the arm, he ordered them to lead him to the red-light district, punctuating every step by a shot which smashed a street light, or struck some wall, a door, or a distant house.

Demetrio left him and returned to the hotel, singing to himself:

> *"Someone plunged a knife*
> *Deep in my side.*
> *Did he know why?*
> *I don't know why.*
> *Maybe he knew,*
> *I never knew."*

XIV

STALE cigarette smoke, the acrid odors of sweaty clothing, the vapors of alcohol, the breathing of a crowded multitude, worse by far than a trainful of pigs.

Texas hats, adorned with gold braid, and khaki predominate. "Gentlemen, a well-dressed man stole my suitcase in the station. My life's savings! I haven't enough to feed my little boy now!"

The shrill voice, rising to a shriek or trailing off into a sob, is drowned out by the tumult within the train.

"What the hell is the old woman talking about?" Blondie asks, entering in search of a seat.

"Something about a suitcase . . . and a well-dressed man," Pancracio replies. He has already the laps of two civilians to sit on.

Demetrio and the others elbow their way in. Since those on whom Pancracio had sat preferred to stand up, Demetrio and Luis Cervantes quickly seize the vacant seats.

Suddenly a woman who has stood up holding a child all the way from Irapuato, faints. A civilian takes the child in his arms. The others pretend to have seen nothing. Some women, traveling with the soldiers, occupy two or three seats with baggage, dogs, cats, parrots. Some of the men wearing Texan hats laugh at the plump arms and pendulous breasts of the woman who fainted.

"Gentlemen, a well-dressed man stole my suitcase at the station in Silao! All my life's savings . . . I haven't got enough to feed my little boy now! . . ."

The old woman speaks rapidly, parrotlike, sighing and sobbing. Her sharp eyes peer about on all sides. Here she gets a bill, and further on, another. They shower money upon her. She finishes the collection, and goes a few seats ahead.

126

"Gentlemen, a well-dressed man stole my suitcase in the station at Silao." Her words produce an immediate and certain effect.

A well-dressed man, a dude, a tenderfoot, stealing a suitcase! Amazing, phenomenal! It awakens a feeling of universal indignation. It's a pity: if this well-dressed man were here every one of the generals would shoot him, one after the other!

"There's nothing as vile as a city dude who steals!" a man says, exploding with indignation.

"To rob a poor old lady!"

"To steal from a poor defenseless woman!"

They prove their compassion by word and deed: a harsh verdict against the culprit; a five-peso bill for the victim.

"And I'm telling you the truth," Blondie declares. "Don't think it's wrong to kill, because when you kill, it's always out of anger. But stealing—Bah!"

This profound piece of reasoning meets with unanimous assent. After a short silence while he meditates, a colonel ventures his opinion:

"Everything is all right according to something, see? That is, everything has its circumstances, see? God's own truth is this: I have stolen, and if I say that everyone here has done the trick, I'm not telling a lie, I reckon!"

"Hell, I stole a lot of them sewing machines in Mexico," exclaims a major. "I made more'n five hundred pesos even though I sold them at fifty cents apiece!"

A toothless captain, with hair prematurely white, announces:

"I stole some horses in Zacatecas, all damn fine horses they was, and then I says to myself, 'This is your own little lottery, Pascual Mata,' I says. 'You won't have a worry in all your life after this.' And the damned thing about it was that General Limón took a fancy to the horses too, and he stole them from me!"

"Of course—there's no use denying it, I've stolen too," Blondie confesses. "But ask any one of my partners how much profit I've got. I'm a big spender and my purse is my friends' to have a good time on! I have a better time if I drink myself senseless than I would have sending money back home to the old woman!"

The subject of "I stole," though apparently inexhaustible, ceases to hold the men's attention. Decks of cards gradually appear on the seats, drawing generals and officers as the light draws mosquitoes.

The excitement of gambling soon absorbs every interest, the heat grows more and more intense. To breathe is to inhale the air of barracks, prison, brothel, and pigsty all in one.

And rising above the babble, from the car ahead ever the shrill voice, "Gentlemen, a well-dressed young man stole . . ."

The streets in Aguascalientes were so many refuse piles. Men in khaki moved to and fro like bees before their hive, overrunning the restaurants, the crapulous lunch houses, the parlous hotels, and the stands of the street vendors on which rotten pork lay alongside grimy cheese.

The smell of these viands whetted the appetites of Demetrio and his men. They forced their way into a small inn, where a disheveled old hag served, on earthenware plates, some pork with bones swimming in a clear chili stew and three tough burnt tortillas. They paid two pesos apiece; as they left Pancracio assured his comrades he was hungrier than when he entered.

"Now," said Demetrio, "we'll go and consult with General Natera!"

They made for the northern leader's billet.

A noisy, excited crowd stopped them at a street crossing. A man, lost in the multitude, was mouthing words in the monotonous, unctuous tones of a prayer. They came up close enough to see him distinctly; he wore a shirt and trousers of cheap white cloth and was repeating:

"All good Catholics should read this prayer to Christ Our Lord upon the Cross with due devotion. Thus they will be immune from storms and pestilence, famine, and war."

"This man's no fool," said Demetrio smiling.

The man waved a sheaf of printed handbills in his hand and cried:

"A quarter of a peso is all you have to pay for this prayer to Christ Our Lord upon the Cross. A quarter . . ."

Then he would duck for a moment, to reappear with a snake's tooth, a sea star, or the skeleton of a fish. In the same predicant tone, he lauded the medical virtues and the mystical powers of every article he sold.

Quail, who had no faith in Venancio, requested the man to pull a tooth out. Blondie purchased a black seed from a certain fruit which protected the possessor from lightning or any other catastrophe. Anastasio Montáñez purchased a prayer to Christ Our Lord upon the Cross, and, folding it carefully, stuck it into his shirt with a pious gesture.

"As sure as there's a God in heaven," Natera said, "this mess hasn't blown over yet. Now it's Villa fighting Carranza."

Without answering him, his eyes fixed in a stare, Demetrio demanded a further explanation.

"It means," Natera said, "that the Convention won't recognize Carranza as First Chief of the Constitutionalist Army. It's going to elect a Provisional President of the Republic. Do you understand me, General?"

Demetrio nodded assent.

"What's your opinion, General?" asked Natera.

Demetrio shrugged his shoulders:

"It seems to me that the meat of the matter is that we've got to go on fighting, eh? All right! Let's go to it! I'm game to the end, you know."

"Good, but on what side?"

Demetrio, nonplussed, scratched his head:

"Look here, don't ask me any more questions. I never went to school, you know. . . . You gave me the eagle I wear on my hat, didn't you? All right then; you just tell me: 'Demetrio, do this or do that,' and that's all there's to it!"

PART THREE

"Villa? Obregón? Carranza? What's the difference? I love the revolution like a volcano in eruption; I love the volcano, because it's a volcano, the revolution, because it's the revolution!"

I

MY DEAR VENANCIO:

Due to the pressure of professional duties I have been unable to answer your letter of January 4 before now. As you already know, I was graduated last December. I was sorry to hear of Pancracio's and Manteca's fate, though I am not surprised that they stabbed each other over the gambling table. It is a pity; they were both brave men. I am deeply grieved not to be able to tell Blondie how sincerely and heartily I congratulate him for the only noble and beautiful thing he ever did in his whole life: to have shot himself!

Dear Venancio, although you may have enough money to purchase a degree, I am afraid you won't find it very easy to become a doctor in this country. You know I like you very much, Venancio; and I think you deserve a better fate. But I have an idea which may prove profitable to both of us and which may improve your social position, as you desire. We could do a fine business here if we were to go in as partners and set up a typical Mexican restaurant in this town. I have no reserve funds at the moment since I've spent all I had in getting my college degree, but I have something much more valuable than money; my perfect knowledge of this town and its needs. You can appear as the owner; we will make a monthly division of profits. Besides, concerning a question that interests us both very much, namely, your social improvement, it occurs to me that you play the guitar quite well. In view of the recommendations I could give you and in view of your train-

132

ing as well, you might easily be admitted as a member of some fraternal order; there are several here which would bring you no inconsiderable social prestige.

Don't hesitate, Venancio, come at once and bring your funds. I promise you we'll get rich in no time. My best wishes to the General, to Anastasio, and the rest of the boys.

Your affectionate friend,
LUIS CERVANTES

Venancio finished reading the letter for the hundredth time and, sighing, repeated:

"Tenderfoot certainly knows how to pull the strings all right!"

"What I can't get into my head," observed Anastasio Montáñez, "is why we keep on fighting. Didn't we finish off this man Huerta and his Federation?"

Neither the General nor Venancio answered; but the same thought kept beating down on their dull brains like a hammer on an anvil.

They ascended the steep hill, their heads bowed, pensive, their horses walking at a slow gait. Stubbornly restless, Anastasio made the same observation to other groups; the soldiers laughed at his candor. If a man has a rifle in his hands and a beltful of cartridges, surely he should use them. That means fighting. Against whom? For whom? That is scarcely a matter of importance.

The endless wavering column of dust moved up the trail, a swirling ant heap of broad straw sombreros, dirty khaki, faded blankets, and black horses. . . .

Not a man but was dying of thirst; no pool or stream or well anywhere along the road. A wave of dust rose from the white, wild sides of a small canyon, swayed mistily on the hoary crest of *huizache* trees and the greenish stumps of cactus. Like a jest, the flowers in the cactus opened out, fresh, solid, aflame, some thorny, others diaphanous.

At noon they reached a hut, clinging to the precipitous sierra, then three more huts strewn over the margin of a river of burnt sand. Everything was silent, desolate. As soon as they saw men on horseback, the people in the huts scurried into the hills to hide. Demetrio grew indignant.

"Bring me anyone you find hiding or running away," he commanded in a loud voice.

"What? What did you say?" Valderrama cried in surprise. "The men of the sierra? Those brave men who've not yet done what those chickens down in Aguascalientes and Zacatecas have done all the time? Our own brothers, who weather storms, who cling to the rocks like moss itself? I protest, sir; I protest!"

He spurred his miserable horse forward and caught up with the General.

"The mountaineers," he said solemnly and emphatically, "are flesh of our flesh, bone of our bone. *Os ex osibus meis et caro de carne mea.* Mountaineers are made from the same timber we're made of! Of the same sound timber from which heroes . . ."

With a confidence as sudden as it was courageous, he hit the General across the chest. The General smiled benevolently.

Valderrama, the tramp, the crazy maker of verses, did he ever know what he said?

When the soldiers reached a small ranch, despairingly, they searched the empty huts and small houses without finding a single stale tortilla, a solitary rotten pepper, or one pinch of salt with which to flavor the horrible taste of dry meat. The owners of the huts, their peaceful brethren, were impassive with the stonelike impassivity of Aztec idols; others, more human, with a slow smile on their colorless lips and beardless faces, watched these fierce men who less than a month ago had made the miserable huts of others tremble with fear, now in their turn fleeing their own huts where the ovens were cold and the water tanks dry, fleeing with their tails between their legs, cringing, like curs kicked out of their own houses.

But the General did not countermand his order. Some soldiers brought back four fugitives, captive and bound.

II

W HY do you hide?" Demetrio asked the prisoners.

"We're not hiding, Chief, we're hitting the trail."

"Where to?"

"To our own homes, in God's name, to Durango."

"Is this the road to Durango?"

"Peaceful people can't travel over the main road nowadays, you know that, Chief."

"You're not peaceful people, you're deserters. Where do you come from?" Demetrio said, eyeing them with keen scrutiny.

The prisoners grew confused; they looked at each other hesitatingly, unable to give a prompt answer.

"They're Carranzistas," one of the soldiers said.

"Carranzistas hell!" one of them said proudly. "I'd rather be a pig."

"The truth is we're deserters," another said. "After the defeat we deserted from General Villa's troops this side of Celaya."

"General Villa defeated? Ha! Ha! That's a good joke."

The soldiers laughed. But Demetrio's brow was wrinkled as though a black shadow had passed over his eyes.

"There ain't a son of a bitch on earth who can beat General Villa!" said a bronzed veteran with a scar clear across the face.

Without a change of expression, one of the deserters stared persistently at him and said:

"I know who you are. When we took Torreón you were with General Urbina. In Zacatecas you were with General Natera and then you shifted to the Jalisco troops. Am I lying?"

These words met with a sudden and definite effect. The prisoners gave a detailed account of the tremendous

135

defeat of Villa at Celaya. Demetrio's men listened in silence, stupefied.

Before resuming their march, they built a fire on which to roast some bull meat. Anastasio Montáñez, searching for food among the *huizache* trees, descried the close-cropped neck of Valderrama's horse in the distance among the rocks.

"Hey! Come here, you fool, after all there ain't been no gravy!" he shouted.

Whenever anything was said about shooting someone, Valderrama, the romantic poet, would disappear for a whole day.

Hearing Anastasio's voice, Valderrama was convinced that the prisoners had been set at liberty. A few moments later, he was joined by Venancio and Demetrio.

"Heard the news?" Venancio asked gravely.

"No."

"It's very serious. A terrible mess! Villa was beaten at Celaya by Obregón and Carranza is winning all along the line! We're done for!"

Valderrama's gesture was disdainful and solemn as an emperor's. "Villa? Obregón? Carranza? What's the difference? I love the revolution like a volcano in eruption; I love the volcano because it's a volcano, the revolution because it's the revolution! What do I care about the stones left above or below after the cataclysm? What are they to me?"

In the glare of the midday sun the reflection of a white tequila bottle glittered on his forehead; and, jubilant, he ran toward the bearer of such a marvelous gift.

"I like this crazy fool," Demetrio said with a smile. "He says things sometimes that make you think."

They resumed their march; their uncertainty translated into a lugubrious silence. Slowly, inevitably, the catastrophe must come; it was even now being realized. Villa defeated was a fallen god; when gods cease to be omnipotent, they are nothing.

Quail spoke. His words faithfully interpreted the general opinion:

"What the hell, boys! Every spider's got to spin his own web now!"

III

In Zacatecas and Aguascalientes, in the little country towns and the neighboring communities, haciendas and ranches were deserted. When one of the officers found a barrel of tequila, the event assumed miraculous proportions. Everything was conducted with secrecy and care; deep mystery was preserved to oblige the soldiers to leave on the morrow before sunrise under Anastasio and Venancio.

When Demetrio awoke to the strains of music, his general staff, now composed chiefly of young ex-government officers, told him of the discovery, and Quail, interpreting the thoughts of his colleagues, said sententiously:

"These are bad times and you've got to take advantage of everythin'. If there are some days when a duck can swim, there's others when he can't take a drink."

The string musicians played all day; the most solemn honors were paid to the barrel: but Demetrio was very sad.

"Did he know why?
I don't know why."

He kept repeating the same refrain.

In the afternoon there were cockfights. Demetrio sat down with the chief officers under the roof of the municipal portals in front of a city square covered with weeds, a tumbled kiosk, and some abandoned adobe houses.

"Valderrama," Demetrio called, looking away from the ring with tired eyes, "come and sing me a song—sing 'The Undertaker.'"

But Valderrama did not hear him; he had no eyes

137

for the fight; he was reciting an impassioned soliloquy as he watched the sunset over the hills.

With solemn gestures and emphatic tones, he said:

"O Lord, Lord, pleasurable it is this thy land! I shall build me three tents: one for Thee, one for Moses, one for Elijah!"

"Valderrama," Demetrio shouted again. "Come and sing 'The Undertaker' song for me."

"Hey, crazy, the General is calling you," an officer shouted.

Valderrama with his eternally complacent smile went over to Demetrio's seat and asked the musicians for a guitar.

"Silence," the gamesters cried. Valderrama finished tuning his instrument.

Quail and Meco let loose on the sand a pair of cocks armed with long sharp blades attached to their legs. One was light red; his feathers shone with beautiful obsidian glints. The other was sand-colored with feathers like scales burned slowly to a fiery copper color.

The fight was swift and fierce as a duel between men. As though moved by springs, the roosters flew at each other. Their feathers stood up on their arched necks; their combs were erect, their legs taut. For an instant they swung in the air without even touching the ground, their feathers, beaks, and claws lost in a dizzy whirlwind. The red rooster suddenly broke, tossed with his legs to heaven outside the chalk lines. His vermilion eyes closed slowly, revealing eyelids of pink coral; his tangled feathers quivered and shook convulsively amid a pool of blood.

Valderrama, who could not repress a gesture of violent indignation, began to play. With the first melancholy strains of the tune, his anger disappeared. His eyes gleamed with the light of madness. His glance strayed over the square, the tumbled kiosk, the old adobe houses, over the mountains in the background, and over the sky, burning like a roof afire. He began to sing. He put such feeling into his voice and such expression into the strings that, as he finished, Demetrio turned his head aside to hide his tears.

But Valderrama fell upon him, embraced him warmly,

and with a familiarity he showed everyone at the appropriate moment, he whispered:

"Drink them! . . . Those are beautiful tears."

Demetrio asked for the bottle, passed it to Valderrama. Greedily the poet drank half its contents in one gulp; then, showing only the whites of his eyes, he faced the spectators dramatically and, in a highly theatrical voice, cried:

"Here you may witness the blessings of the revolution caught in a single tear."

Then he continued to talk like a madman, but like a madman whose vast prophetic madness encompassed all about him, the dusty weeds, the tumbled kiosk, the gray houses, the lovely hills, and the immeasurable sky.

IV

JUCHIPILA rose in the distance, white, bathed in sunlight, shining in the midst of a thick forest at the foot of a proud, lofty mountain, pleated like a turban.

Some of the soldiers, gazing at the spire of the church, sighed sadly. They marched forward through the canyon, uncertain, unsteady, as blind men walking without a hand to guide them. The bitterness of the exodus pervaded them.

"Is that town Juchipila?" Valderrama asked.

In the first stage of his drunkenness, Valderrama had been counting the crosses scattered along the road, along the trails, in the hollows near the rocks, in the tortuous paths, and along the riverbanks. Crosses of black timber newly varnished, makeshift crosses built out of two logs, crosses of stones piled up and plastered together, crosses whitewashed on crumbling walls, humble crosses drawn with charcoal on the surface of whitish rocks. The traces of the first blood shed by the revolutionists of 1910, murdered by the Government.

Before Juchipila was lost from sight, Valderrama got off his horse, bent down, kneeled, and gravely kissed the ground.

The soldiers passed by without stopping. Some laughed at the crazy man, others jested. Valderrama, deaf to all about him, breathed his unctuous prayer:

"O Juchipila, cradle of the Revolution of 1910, O blessed land, land steeped in the blood of martyrs, blood of dreamers, the only true men . . ."

"Because they had no time to be bad!" an ex-Federal officer interjected as he rode.

Interrupting his prayer, Valderrama frowned, burst into stentorian laughter, reechoed by the rocks, and ran toward the officer begging for a swallow of tequila.

Soldiers minus an arm or leg, cripples, rheumatics, and consumptives spoke bitterly of Demetrio. Young whippersnappers were given officers' commissions and wore stripes on their hats without a day's service, even before they knew how to handle a rifle, while the veterans, exhausted in a hundred battles, now incapacitated for work, the veterans who had set out as simple privates, were still simple privates. The few remaining officers among Demetrio's friends also grumbled, because his staff was made up of wealthy, dapper young men who oiled their hair and used perfume.

"The worst part of it," Venancio said, "is that we're gettin' overcrowded with Federals!"

Anastasio himself, who invariably found only praise for Demetrio's conduct, now seemed to share the general discontent.

"See here, brothers," he said, "I spits out the truth when I sees something. I always tell the boss that if these people stick to us very long we'll be in a hell of a fix. Certainly! How can anyone think otherwise? I've no hair on my tongue; and by the mother that bore me, I'm going to tell Demetrio so myself."

Demetrio listened benevolently, and, when Anastasio had finished, he replied:

"You're right, there's no gettin' around it, we're in a bad way. The soldiers grumble about the officers, the officers grumble about us, see? And we're damn well ready now to send both Villa and Carranza to hell to have a good time all by themselves. . . . I guess we're in the same fix as that peon from Tepatitlán who complained about his boss all day long but worked on just the same. That's us. We kick and kick, but we keep on killing and killing. But there's no use in saying anything to them!"

"Why, Demetrio?"

"Hm, I don't know. . . . Because . . . because . . . do you see? . . . What we've got to do is to make the men toe the mark. I've got orders to stop a band of men coming through Cuquío, see? In a few days we'll have to fight the Carranzistas. It will be great to beat the hell out of them."

Valderrama, the tramp, who had enlisted in Demetrio's army one day without anyone remembering the time or the place, overheard some of Demetrio's words. Fools do not eat fire. That very day Valderrama disappeared mysteriously as he had come.

V

THEY entered the streets of Juchipila as the church bells rang, loud and joyfully, with that peculiar tone that thrills every mountaineer.

"It makes me think we are back in the days when the revolution was just beginning, when the bells rang like mad in every town we entered and everybody came out with music, flags, cheers, and fireworks to welcome us," said Anastasio Montáñez.

"They don't like us no more," Demetrio returned.

"Of course. We're crawling back like a dog with its tail between its legs," Quail remarked.

"It ain't that, I guess. They don't give a whoop for the other side either."

"But why should they like us?"

They spoke no more.

Presently they reached the city square and stopped in front of an octagonal, rough, massive church, reminiscent of the colonial period. At one time the square must have been a garden, judging from the bare stunted orange trees planted between iron and wooden benches. The sonorous, joyful bells rang again. From within the church, the honeyed voices of a female chorus rose melancholy and grave. To the strains of a guitar, the young girls of the town sang the "Mysteries."

"What's the fiesta, lady?" Venancio asked of an old woman who was running toward the church.

"The Sacred Heart of Jesus!" answered the pious woman, panting.

They remembered that one year ago they had captured Zacatecas. They grew sadder still.

Juchipila, like the other towns they had passed through on their way from Tepic, by way of Jalisco, Aguascalientes and Zacatecas, was in ruins. The black trail of the incendiaries showed in the roofless houses, in the burnt arcades. Almost all the houses were closed, yet, here and there, those still open offered, in ironic contrast, portals gaunt and bare as the white skeletons of horses scattered over the roads. The terrible pangs of hunger seemed to speak from every face; hunger on every dusty cheek, in their dusty countenances; in the hectic flame of their eyes, which, when they met a soldier, blazed with hatred. In vain the soldiers scoured the streets in search of food, biting their lips in anger. A single lunchroom was open; at once they filled it. No beans, no tortillas, only chili and tomato sauce. In vain the officers showed their pocketbooks stuffed with bills or used threats:

"Yea, you've got papers all right! That's all you've brought! Try and eat them, will you?" said the owner, an insolent old shrew with an enormous scar on her cheek, who told them she had already lain with a dead man, "to cure her from ever feeling frightened again."

Despite the melancholy and desolation of the town, while the women sang in the church, birds sang in the foliage, and the thrushes piped their lyrical strain on the withered branches of the orange trees.

VI

DEMETRIO MACÍAS' wife, mad with joy, rushed along the trail to meet him, leading a child by the hand.

An absence of almost two years!

They embraced each other and stood speechless. She wept, sobbed. Demetrio stared in astonishment at his wife who seemed to have aged ten or twenty years. Then he looked at the child who gazed up at him in surprise. His heart leaped to his mouth as he saw in the child's features his own steel features and fiery eyes exactly reproduced. He wanted to hold him in his arms, but the frightened child took refuge in his mother's skirts.

"It's your own father, baby! It's your daddy!"

The child hid his face within the folds of his mother's skirt, still hostile.

Demetrio handed the reins of his horse to his orderly and walked slowly along the steep trail with his wife and son.

"Blessed be the Virgin Mary, Praise be to God! Now you'll never leave us any more, will you? Never . . . never. . . . You'll stay with us always?"

Demetrio's face grew dark. Both remained silent, lost in anguish. Demetrio suppressed a sigh. Memories crowded and buzzed through his brain like bees about a hive.

A black cloud rose behind the sierra and a deafening roar of thunder resounded. The rain began to fall in heavy drops; they sought refuge in a rocky hut.

The rain came pelting down, shattering the white Saint John roses clustered like sheaves of stars clinging to tree, rock, bush, and *pitaya* over the entire mountainside.

Below in the depths of the canyon, through the gauze of the rain they could see the tall, sheer palms shaking in the wind, opening out like fans before the tempest.

Everywhere mountains, heaving hills, and beyond more hills, locked amid mountains, more mountains encircled in the wall of the sierra whose loftiest peaks vanished in the sapphire of the sky.

"Demetrio, please. For God's sake, don't go away! My heart tells me something will happen to you this time."

Again she was wracked with sobs. The child, frightened, cried and screamed. To calm him, she controlled her own great grief.

Gradually the rain stopped, a swallow, with silver breast and wings describing luminous charming curves, fluttered obliquely across the silver threads of the rain, gleaming suddenly in the afternoon sunshine.

"Why do you keep on fighting, Demetrio?"

Demetrio frowned deeply. Picking up a stone absent-mindedly, he threw it to the bottom of the canyon. Then he stared pensively into the abyss, watching the arch of its flight.

"Look at that stone; how it keeps on going. . . ."

VII

IT was a heavenly morning. It had rained all night, the sky awakened covered with white clouds. Young wild colts trotted on the summit of the sierra, with tense manes and waving hair, proud as the peaks lifting their heads to the clouds.

The soldiers stepped among the huge rocks, buoyed up by the happiness of the morning. None for a moment dreamed of the treacherous bullet that might be awaiting him ahead; the unforeseen provides man with his greatest joy. The soldiers sang, laughed, and chattered away. The spirit of nomadic tribes stirred their souls. What matters it whither you go and whence you come? All that matters is to walk, to walk endlessly, without ever stopping; to possess the valley, the heights of the sierra, far as the eye can read.

Trees, brush, and cactus shone fresh after rain. Heavy drops of limpid water fell from rocks, ocher in hue as rusty armor.

Demetrio Macías' men grew silent for a moment. They believed they heard the familiar rumor of firing in the distance. A few minutes elapsed but the sound was not repeated.

"In this same sierra," Demetrio said, "with but twenty men I killed five hundred Federals. Remember, Anastasio?"

As Demetrio began to tell that famous exploit, the men realized the danger they were facing. What if the enemy, instead of being two days away, was hiding somewhere among the underbrush on the terrible hill through whose gorge they now advanced? None dared show the slightest fear. Not one of Demetrio Macías' men dared say, "I shall not move another inch!"

So, when firing began in the distance where the vanguard was marching, no one felt surprised. The recruits turned back hurriedly, retreating in shameful flight, searching for a way out of the canyon.

A curse broke from Demetrio's parched lips.

"Fire at 'em. Shoot any man who runs away!"

"Storm the hill!" he thundered like a wild beast.

But the enemy, lying in ambush by the thousand, opened up its machine-gun fire. Demetrio's men fell like wheat under the sickle.

Tears of rage and pain rise to Demetrio's eyes as Anastasio slowly slides from his horse without a sound, and lies outstretched, motionless. Venancio falls close beside him, his chest riddled with bullets. Meco hurtles over the precipice, bounding from rock to rock.

Suddenly, Demetrio finds himself alone. Bullets whiz past his ears like hail. He dismounts and crawls over the rocks, until he finds a parapet: he lays down a stone to protect his head and, lying flat on the ground, begins to shoot.

The enemy scatter in all directions, pursuing the few fugitives hiding in the brush. Demetrio aims; he does not waste a single shot.

His famous marksmanship fills him with joy. Where he settles his glance, he settles a bullet. He loads his gun once more . . . takes aim. . . .

The smoke of the guns hangs thick in the air. Locusts chant their mysterious, imperturbable song. Doves coo lyrically in the crannies of the rocks. The cows graze placidly.

The sierra is clad in gala colors. Over its inaccessible peaks the opalescent fog settles like a snowy veil on the forehead of a bride.

At the foot of a hollow, sumptuous and huge as the portico of an old cathedral, Demetrio Macías, his eyes leveled in an eternal glance, continues to point the barrel of his gun.

SELECTED BIBLIOGRAPHY

OTHER WORKS BY MARIANO AZUELA

Los fracasados, 1908   Novel
Mala yerba, 1909   Novel
Andrés Pérez, maderista, 1911   Novel
Sin amor, 1912   Novel
Los caciques, 1917   Novel
Las moscas, 1918   Novel
Domitilo quiere ser diputado, 1918   Novel
Las tribulaciones de una familia decente, 1918   Novel
La luciérnaga, 1932   Novel
El camarada Pantoja, 1937   Novel
San Gabriel de Valdivia, 1938   Novel
La marchanta, 1944   Novel
Obras completas (Complete Works), 1958 Vols. I and II;
1959 Vol. III

SELECTED BIOGRAPHY AND CRITICISM

Beals, Carleton. *Mexican Maze.* Philadelphia: J. B. Lippincott &
Co., Inc., 1931.

Brenner, Anita. *Idols behind Altars.* New York: Harcourt, Brace &
Co., Inc., 1929.

Gamboa de Camino, Berta. *The Novel of the Mexican Revolution.*
New York: Renascent Mexico, 1935.